After a fall of society the g[ood,] fearing people will be faced [with killing] themselves or their loved ones to survive. Many will shrink from it. But those with wives or children will not stand by and watch them starve to death - slowly, horribly, painfully!

Whereas before the fall of civilization those good people might "brake for animals," now they might have to kill those animals to eat, and then kill other humans, to defend themselves and their families. Once they come to grips with it, and kill something for the first time, they might find that it wasn't so terrible after all. They might find that squirrel actually tastes like chicken!

Humans, on the other hand, do not, and will not submit themselves as easily as squirrels. You might never have to kill anybody, but are easily a fool if not prepared to. I will help you become prepared. I guarantee it's not as hard as you may think.

-Doomsday Marauders, Getting Your Gameface On

It's been said "you never feel so alive as when you're close to death." Well, that's a bunch of shit! When I've been close to death I didn't smell any flowers, catch the taste of wild grasses on the breeze, noticed how beautiful the blue sky is, or any of that crap! I've usually smelled gunpowder, oil, the dirt my face is smashed down in, somebody's ass if my head's buried in it, fighting to the death, tasted blood in my mouth, the seawater I'm drowning in or have seen, extremely clearly, the sunlight, glinting off the instrument of my death, either a 9mm or a sharp blade- So trust me, when you're very close to death, it's extremely stressful. And it completely sucks!

-Doomsday Marauders, Chapter Eight – Taking Out a Well-Defended Ranch

DOOMSDAY
MARAUDERS

DOOMSDAY MARAUDERS

KILKENNY

AuthorHouse™ LLC
1663 Liberty Drive
Bloomington, IN 47403
www.authorhouse.com
Phone: 1-800-839-8640

© 2014 Kilkenny. All rights reserved.

No part of this book may be reproduced, stored in a retrieval system, or transmitted by any means without the written permission of the author.

Published by AuthorHouse 05/06/2014

ISBN: 978-1-4969-0767-7 (sc)
ISBN: 978-1-4969-0766-0 (hc)
ISBN: 978-1-4969-0765-3 (e)

Library of Congress Control Number: 2014907871

Any people depicted in stock imagery provided by Thinkstock are models, and such images are being used for illustrative purposes only.
Certain stock imagery © Thinkstock.

This book is printed on acid-free paper.

Because of the dynamic nature of the Internet, any web addresses or links contained in this book may have changed since publication and may no longer be valid. The views expressed in this work are solely those of the author and do not necessarily reflect the views of the publisher, and the publisher hereby disclaims any responsibility for them.

This book is dedicated to my Dad, an 81 year-old Marine whose influence extends far beyond me, and my siblings, down through my twin girls and onward to my son, another Marine Corps officer. What he did for me, and what he taught me, has helped keep me alive and even thrive in making it this far. I'm sure he has no idea of the extent to which his attitudes and examples have affected me, to this day still. A more mentally tough human does not exist. Thanks Dad.

CONTENTS

My Mission xi
Author's Note xv
About Me xix

1   Apocalyptic Hell—*Why Prepping Won't Work* 1
2   Getting Your Game Face On!—*Practicing For The Next Life* ... 17
3   The Girl from Ipanema—*A True Personal Story* 31
4   The Marauder Toolkit—*Guns. Lots of Guns* 47
5   Marauding 101 —*The How-To's, the 10 Steps and Rules for the Road* 81
6   The Road to Leon'—*Another True Personal Story* 89
7   Taking Out a Lightly Defended Farm—*How it's Done* 105
8   Taking Out A Well-Defended Ranch—*A Higher Degree of Difficulty* 115
9   The Belly of the Sexy Beast *A Very Personal Story* 129
10 Taking Down a Survivalist Colony—*We Get Mean Here* ... 141

Summary—*Random Thoughts On Lessons Learned* 181
How to Survive the Initial Post-Fall Chaos 185
About the Author 197

MY MISSION

My name is Kilkenny, and I wrote the book <u>Doomsday Marauders</u> to challenge and counter all of the propaganda written and advertised out there about surviving doomsday, a fall of civilized society, any disintegration into lawlessness or any other kind of apocalyptic event. I intend to convince anyone smart enough to listen that they've got it all wrong. *Dangerously so.*

If you think that by following the advice from anyone on shows like Doomsday Preppers or Doomsday Castle, you won't last more than ten minutes after a fall of society. That's kid stuff—those shows have done more harm than good to anyone doing serious thinking about what to do, how to survive. *Prepping is not the answer.* Sure, you need to have some supplies on hand to get going, but the only real way to keep living, and *thriving, is by looking for what you need and then taking it.* Everybody else out there will be doing, or trying, the same thing. I'll show you how—Why me? Because I'm the real thing, the original *Marauder*—Read "About Me" if you're serious at all about this subject, or if you have any doubt.

KILKENNY

<u>For all of you Preppers</u>—Think about it—not one single group of people in history has ever withstood a siege. History is littered with the millions of bodies of those who thought they could. From the siege of Masada through the Sieges of Paris and Stalingrad, the well-positioned, well-provisioned and well-armed defenders all lost. A more current example, closer to your own situation, would be the White farmers in Rhodesia. Ultimately overrun by larger numbers of poorly equipped, ridiculously poor, ignorant vagabonds. *They were tortured and killed, women raped, bodies mutilated.* The fact that they had relatively sophisticated defense arrangements, including land mines and radio systems, ultimately meant nothing. It's not like they were up against Navy SEAL's or Marines. They were brutally eliminated by bands of ignorant, savage criminals. The same thing is happening right now to the White farmers in South Africa. Do you think they were ignorant of what happened in Rhodesia? Of course not! They actually thought they had better defenses! *But they've lost, again, badly! Women raped, men tortured, bodies mutilated.*

Are you ready to deal with *that?* The end of civilized society as you know it, and subsequent descent into lawlessness, will not be pretty. It will be *Hell.*

I'm putting everything you need to know out there and up front. My book shows you how you might survive, even *thrive* after the Fall. There's only one way, by being a *Marauder.* Throughout this book I begin to describe what you will face, how you should handle it, and what you will need to do it. This doesn't mean just grabbing a gun and ripping off those idiots on *"Doomsday Preppers,"* or even a simple challenging of the significantly more dangerous, mindless bands of raiders and looters taking stuff and attacking at gunpoint, as I encountered in Liberia and Sierra Leone. I'm talking about professional, systematic and organized operations, many occurring simultaneously, designed to take from others what you need, when you need it. Does this sound harsh to you? *Then wake the hell up!* In that new world out there they will be coming for you, make no mistake. *They will be coming for you and they will find you. They will shoot your dog. They will brutally rape your wife and your daughters. They will burn down your home. They will kill you.* You want that? You think because you bought an AR-15 and a 9mm that you can actually stop them?

There's only one way to survive. Go out and do it first. I will show you how. Read "About Me."

AUTHOR'S NOTE

In writing Doomsday Marauders I've attempted to take some pretty dry subject material (equipment, supplies, weapons, dogs, etc.) and make it more interesting and witty than the average read by incorporating a fiction-like approach to some of the material while maintaining the first-person narrative throughout. The result is that my usually sarcastic and prickly sense of humor comes shining through. You'll see what I mean as you get into the book. My wife says that's its best feature. I don't know how to take that!

I've also added some true stories from some of the events of my personal experiences in the Intelligence world, writing them in the first-person, in real time and hopefully well enough that they come off to you, the reader, as if you actually were reading fiction. I've altered some of the names, of course, for my own protection. Not from violence, but from lawsuits!

Hopefully I haven't bored you to tears early on and you've finally made it to the point in the book where I describe how to conduct realistic operations against farms, ranches and even a survivor colony. I wrote these "how-to's" in the form of fiction as well. I gave you every idea, every action, every detail you need to supply, plan and succeed at any operation, but I also gave you every thought, every communication, setting, setback, change, planning on both sides, etc., to make it read smoother and hopefully more interesting while giving you a more comprehensive picture as to how to conduct these raids with success. I think it's more fun this way rather than just writing "First you get some horses, then you load up your weapons," Wah Wah Wah take one of those weapons and shoot me now if that's the case. Hopefully you'll enjoy this approach much better.

Lastly, this book covers many related, but different, types of material, from weapons to Military to Intelligence to lawlessness, etc. etc. If you know all about handguns, rifles, body armor, explosives, and such, feel free to skip those sections, but I assure you the writing has its moments! The same is true for the little vignettes from my past. If rape and killing upset you, *for God's sake don't read them!* Oh, and I use Italics quite frequently throughout, to let you, the reader, know what's important to me. *For emphasis!*

Lastly, feel free to skip back and forth throughout the book. As long as you've read "About Me" (at least the Short Version) then anywhere at all you pick a page to read you will have an understanding of where I'm coming from, and probably where you're headed as well. I've set up the book so that it can be read this way. If you go right to Takedowns, you should have no problem learning how; but if you find you need additional information about weapons, equipment, etc. to help you understand, you can go back in the book and find it. If you care to start reading about my true-life experiences, feel free to start there as well. They're constructed as independent stories, added to the book to give some real-world examples of how my methods and tactics might apply.

All in all, I hope that you take *something* away from this read. And please share your thoughts by emailing me:

kilkenny@doomsdaymarauders.com

Doomsdaymarauders.com is my website as well. *Enjoy!*

Kilkenny
New York City
April 1, 2014

ABOUT ME...

The Short Version

Born and raised in the Bronx. Graduated Boston College. Played football. Studied martial arts under Grandmaster Bong Soo Han, the "real" Billy Jack. Learned how to kill from the old-school USMC Force Recon. Fluent in Spanish. Successful International Banker. Recruited by the CIA. Twice. Ran operations throughout South America and Western Africa. Recruited by the Mossad. Once. Imprisoned, twice.

The Longer Story

During the late 70's, while still in my junior year at Boston College, I was recruited by the Central Intelligence Agency. The letter came in a plain, white business envelope, with a nondescript, downtown Boston return address printed on it. It inquired as to whether I might be interested in a very exciting and challenging international career, defending America's interests abroad. It suggested that I call the phone number provided. At the time I was not very interested, as my true desire was to become a Marine Corps fighter pilot. I wanted to fly the Harrier. I was curious, though, as to how I wound up on the CIA "list." I came to find out later on that BC was a hotbed of recruiting by the Clandestine Services of the various U.S. intelligence agencies, and my background fit one of their profiles. I tossed the letter into a big brown box with all of my other career information and job applications.

That summer, as it turns out, my 20-20 vision slipped a little bit to 20-25 minus, and as a result I wasn't going to be able to fly Harriers for the Marines. *I was devastated.* My dream had crashed and burned in the blink of an eye, literally. I was lost. For the first time since my eighth birthday, I cried. I had no idea what to do next. Now terribly depressed, I couldn't see myself graduating BC and working a desk job, even though that's what my business school education had trained me for. A job in banking and finance. *I couldn't think of anything more boring.*

Maybe it was Fate, though more likely Desperation, that drove me to search for that envelope I had received months before. The female voice on the other end of the telephone answering machine politely but firmly asked that I leave my name, date and time of call. That was how it began. A year later I was accepted by the CIA as a "Pre-Career Trainee," basically a glorified gopher. It was a new program for young, inexperienced (idiotic but impressionable) college grads. If you made a good impression on somebody, then maybe after two or three years you would be placed in the "Career Training Program," and were sent to the "Farm," the CIA spy and tradecraft school at Camp Peary, Virginia. Everyone in the CIA's Clandestine Service goes through this program. It is ridiculously selective. Some of the smartest and most patriotic Americans on this planet have been through this program. If you did not make an impression, you went home.

On my first day at the Agency I took a battery of medical and psychological tests, followed by the lie detector, which I promptly and unceremoniously, flunked. I lied about smoking pot at BC, having been told by other recruits that I had met during the yearlong interview process that ANY drug use was a no-go and would prevent my employment at the agency. So, when my 22 year-old idiot brain told me to lie, I lied. I thought that if I never, ever caved in that they might believe me, they might think they were making a mistake, the lie detector was giving a false positive, etc. *They kept me in the chair for four hours,* trying to "break" me. At least that's what I stupidly thought. They actually just wanted me to admit the truth, and stay clean for 6 months. I found that out four years later. I was promptly terminated before I really started. I had crashed and burned again. *Again!*

Fast-forward four years and I'm a successful young International Banker, working and travelling frequently between and around the U.S., Mexico, Colombia and Argentina. I had a *very hot* Colombian girlfriend. I spoke fluent Spanish and had no problem wandering around down there. Flying to Miami from Bogota' after a business trip late one night, my first-class seatmate struck up a casual conversation with me. His questions got a little personal, and at first I thought he was gay, and might be hitting on me. *I kept an eye on my cocktail.* Quickly, though I figured it out and started laughing to myself as I connected the dots and realized that *I was being recruited again!* This time the CIA was looking for a true "agent," not an employee. This is somebody who has information, relationships or access that the Intelligence community pays cash for. Apparently the Agency didn't have a lot of access into the Colombian government at the time, whereas I had made some significant contacts in the Colombian government and industry. I debated their offer, and after a few weeks of negotiating I agreed, as long as they would put me through their Paramilitary Program at Harvey Point in North Carolina. I always thought that would be a blast (no pun, really). They said they would, but to do that I needed to get a commission.

I quit my day job, and attended USMC Officer Candidate School at Quantico, Virginia. Upon completion I received a Lieutenant's commission in the U.S. Marine Corps, and drove down to Harvey Point. Six months later I was back working again in a high-paying corporate job, as Vice President in charge of Latin America for one of the world's largest banks.

By day I was successfully arranging legitimate financing for energy and development projects throughout the region, and by night I was funding guerilla activity throughout Latin America, and posing as a banker to drug lords, including soldiers in the army of Pablo Escobar. I was having a blast, making truckloads of money and living a large life in the fastest of fast lanes. I lived by my own rules, dictated my own terms. And I was winning. I had no fear. That would come later-

I was extremely successful in both my banking career and my Agency relationship. So much so that I was asked by the Agency to get to know some people in West Africa. In particular, someone whom I had met a few times while I was living in Boston, a former Bentley College student named Charles Taylor-

As most of you now know, Charles Taylor is one of the most vile mass murderers and war criminals History has ever seen. He tried real hard to rank with Hitler, Stalin, Genghis Khan and Mao. He is currently imprisoned in Holland, awaiting the outcome of an appeal following his trial and conviction by the International Criminal Court of The Hague for Crimes Against Humanity. These occurred during his presidency in Liberia and the ensuing civil wars in Sierra Leone and Liberia. The whole Blood Diamond conflict. That said, at one time Charles Taylor was a valued informant for the CIA and the DIA (Defense Intelligence Agency), particularly regarding the now-deceased Moammar Gadhafi's activity in Libya, and Al Qaeda's activities in Africa. I was asked to go to Liberia on my own and pretend to offer financing for his regime.

What happened there could fill the pages of another book. Maybe I'll write about that one day. For now, all I'll say is that what I experienced there was Hell. *Sierra Leone and Liberia were and still are, Hell.* But that's where I really learned how to survive the true, total breakdown of civilized society. Part training, part Bronx and partly because of some guys at the Hotel Boulevard in Monrovia I made it out alive. Not all bad, though, as we all took a bunch of "souvenirs" home with us. "Souvenirs" are an important theme throughout my book. My ex-wife will be shocked to read here that the giant, emerald-cut rock she still wears on her right hand originally came from Sierra Leone. So did our Picasso. Indirectly. For the rest of you, don't kid yourself that what went on over there was all Taylor's fault. We helped put Taylor in the position to wreak the havoc he did. And De Beers had a *whole* lot to do with it. Yeah, the Diamond people. *Scumbags.* That's what really made me quit that whole life (and the fact that I had stolen enough of their money to actually do it!).

CHAPTER 1

Apocalyptic Hell—
Why Prepping Won't Work

Doomsday Preppers are the 7/11's of a post-apocalyptic U.S. Just like today, *7/11's I will rob and ravage every week!*

If you're reading this book then I'm sure that you've been exposed in some way to the pop phenomenon known as Doomsday Preparedness or "prepping" for short. It has taken over pop culture, given credence to the rise of Zombies, spawned dozens of Alien takeover movies and numerous reality television shows, and has generally become a part of the discussion regarding 'the future'. America, and a good part of the world, has become obsessed with what to do about surviving the Apocalypse, a nuclear or biological war, the collapse of society resulting from overburdened economies, unemployment, civil strife, etc. My own feelings about this were that this had all peaked and passed when the Mayan 'prophecy' did not come about in December of 2012. I was wrong. That was only the beginning. A good deal of money is now being made in this new "industry" of Doomsday Preparedness. The sad truth, though, is that *most of it is a colossal waste of money.* Think about the premise behind all of this for just a second. *Surviving Doomsday.* That's an oxymoron. Let's look at the possibilities. Forget about surviving all-out nuclear war between any country possessing nuclear weapons and the U.S. I'm not referring to the ridiculous amount of destruction that will occur here, but *the fallout.* Radioactive fallout and practical fallout. It will kill off most living things, and the nuclear winter that will follow will finish off the rest. Don't waste your money on fallout shelters. There will be nuclear fallout contaminating just about everything for a lot longer than the two weeks that the "experts" tell you. The same is true for an all-out biological war. Although the infrastructure and climate may remain intact, a dedicated effort to kill humans with bugs or viruses cannot be contained. If you query any reasonably respected epidemiologists, they will tell you that most naturally occurring bugs and viruses do, in fact, mutate. But unlike the harmless mutations that ultimately occur in movies like "The Andromeda Strain" or "Contagion," *they mutate into more efficient killers!* We've already witnessed on a very low-level what something like SARS can do. Imagine how deadly something created by the Defense Department might be.

What about Doomsday preppers?

They use terms like "TEOTWAWKI" (the end of the world as we know it) or "TSHTF" (the shit hits the fan) and "GOOD" (get out of Dodge)! Some go on to deliberately and specifically describe what they will do when this happens. *Pay no attention to any of that crap! Toss out any old information you have about this or these silly acronyms you might have seen or read about.* If the electric and gas utility grid goes down, maybe never to come back up again, and there ensues a total collapse of organized, government services and society, the result will not be an acronym. *It will be an exclamation point !*

What do I mean by this?

Literally the end of civilization. No acronyms, no cute phrases like "bug-out bag," "G.O.O.D vehicles" or "prepped and ready." It will mean the ugly, slow, torturous death of the human race. This event is by no means a joke. There won't be any curiosity about "what the future holds" or what the "new world" will look like. *It will be Hell.* It will be loneliness, disease, starvation, and painful death. The stench in some places will be overwhelming. A world without Internet, mass communication, television, news, or entertainment. No emergency medical care. There will be theft, murder and all sorts of atrocities. Rape on a colossal scale. Immense suffering, psychosis and mass suicide. Despite this horror, some of us will survive, of course. *Some of us will even thrive*. But the starkest, most terrifying truth however, is that half of us will be dead after one year, and the half of us that remain after one year will be dead by the end of two, and by the end of year three only about 12% of the population that existed before the Fall of Civilization will remain. Humanity, as a species and over the long haul, will ultimately succumb.

So what are people preparing for?

Well, most of these people are preparing for things that are not survivable. That said, however, an event that takes down the grid for an extended period, say, a terrorist attack killing the

President and Congress, or the joint Chiefs, etc. or the collapse of financial markets spilling millions into the streets in protest could result in the loss of services for many, many months. That, in reality, might make it permanent. If the supply chain gets disrupted for that long, *that's the end.* We all live our lives 'knowing' there will be food in the stores, water when we turn on the tap, and light when we flip the switch. Without supply chain, it all falls apart. In a true disaster, military personnel will man civilian stations and take over some civilian tasks only for as long as they are supplied. As I will say again later in this book, it's good news that you have an army, bad news that you actually have to feed it—All posts, held by anyone, will be abandoned after a few days without supplies, especially when those manning them have families at risk.

So certain Doomsday survival scenarios are reasonable?

The answer is yes—the real question is *for how long?* Will the government and the Military be able to hold itself together for three months, six months or even a year and begin to re-establish civil society? Nobody knows that answer. I'm sure that our top officials *think* they can. The reality may be somewhat different. For the general population at large, however, faced almost overnight with no utilities, no communication, no readily available food supply, etc. the outlook is chilling. And in all probability unsurvivable.

Why do I say 'unsurvivable?'

Again, if you're reading this book you've probably read other doomsday material, watched a reality show or movie or maybe saw an article or two about survival after the fall of society. You probably already know that we humans can live for weeks without food, but only a few days without water. Think about it—*only a few days without water!* Think about it again because up to this point I'm sure you've not thought much about it at all. 'Maybe I'll get a filter' or 'I'll boil my water' is the level to which your thinking has probably taken you. If that's the case then you're dead already, along with about 25% of the population that will run out of clean water relatively quickly (within a few weeks). Why? Try one weekend without using household, utility-provided clean water or bottled water and drinks. You will find, especially if you have a family, that providing fresh, clean water is almost a full-time task. This is true also when nobody else is competing with you for that resource, it is as safe and comfortable as ever to wander around town, and there is no psychological terror that will come with the realization that if you fail, you die. Are you feeling this yet?

No?

If you live on a farm, or way out in the country and are supplied by water from your own well, congratulations. You survive the first few weeks. Needless to say, however, if you live in a high-rise apartment or condo in a big city, you're probably immediately doomed. For now, let's assume you live in a home in suburbia, and for argument's sake, maybe you can find a water source nearby, or close enough to manage a few trips hauling small containers back and forth to your home. Water is heavy, isn't it? Okay, now what? Try boiling it on your propane-powered gas stove, as your utility does not provide gas to your kitchen stove anymore. It takes a while to boil all that water, or pump it through that little backpacking filter, then load all of that fresh, clean water into clean containers, right? Imagine having to do this *almost every day!* Hopefully now you can begin to understand the extreme difficulty in *managing only drinking water,* the primary necessity after the Fall of Civilization, and I haven't even addressed water supplies to be used for washing, cleaning or for general sanitation. Clearly, you will find, it takes a very dedicated and disciplined effort on the part of all family members to continually manage a consistently clean water supply. Many of us will not be up to the task. And for those who are not, *many will attempt to take clean water from those of us who are.*

What now?

Okay, you've spent a good part of your day securing a consistent, clean water supply. *Are you hungry yet?* Although the human body can survive for weeks without food, in reality, if someone does not provide food to that human body after a week or so, *it will become too weak at that point to go out and find some!* Assuming that your local Stop N' Shop, Safeway, Albertson's or Winn-Dixie has been completely emptied after a day or two, what's the plan for finding food? Don't have one? Well, you're part of that unlucky first 50% who don't make it. You have food supplies and "staples" in your pantry? Well then, maybe you have a couple of weeks added to your life expectancy. After that, then what? You won't be able to grow food or raise chickens in a couple of weeks, so back to square one. What's the plan?

It's extremely hard obtaining a clean water supply, but obtaining edible food requires an even greater effort. We are so far removed as a society from even our grandparents only a hundred years ago when it comes to providing, acquiring and storing food that it is useless to even think about it. We give no thought as to how it arrives in our kitchen. We open a can, pop a bag into the microwave, or stick a semi-prepared dish in the oven. Suddenly now, the *only* system of food production, processing and delivery to our homes that we've ever known has now been permanently disrupted. Guess what—It's time to invent a new system.

Take it from someone else.

That's right. You read that correctly. *Take it from someone else.* Would you stand by and let your children or your wife or your parents or your siblings die a slow, miserable death from starvation? Most of us would not. You will take extreme measures. You will justify the act of stealing in order to save your family. Get used to it, as everyone else out there will be thinking the same thing. It's up to you, though, to do it better, and to avoid being the one getting taken from, in the process of learning how. You will learn how in this book.

At this point maybe you're dismissing what you've just read because you're a "prepper" and you've got potable water, sufficient food supplies and other things stored safely and securely away, maybe even enough to last a whole year. That's great. Maybe you might get lucky and prolong the inevitable. Or maybe you get luckier, and the grid magically comes back up after a few months, civil order is restored, and you've managed to hide out someplace where nobody could find you. Great. But if the grid doesn't come back up, what's your plan when you run out of food and water? You've been pretty cozy there snacking and hiding out while the rest of the world struggled. Now you're a little late to the party—those survivors out there, where you were not, somehow figured out a way to make it, while you haven't had to. How will you compete with them? Worse yet, what happens if you get discovered after a month or so, when society as it exists is past the desperation point? I'll tell you what-

They will kill you and take your stuff.

They will. Absolutely. History repeats itself, and this has always been the result, horrifically demonstrated over and over again in every war-torn or post-conflict society where government services and security are no longer provided, electric power and transportation systems are gone and the rule of law does not apply. Think Rwanda. Think Blood Diamonds. For those of you skeptics who believe that this type of civil disintegration is only possible in Africa, think about the breakup of Yugoslavia, and the Balkans—That was Eastern Europe. Modern civilized society. I know. I was there.

So now, are you really ready for them? 24 hours a day ready? *Ready to be at Def Con 1 for the remainder of your existence?* Maybe you think you are. You have rifles and handguns. You have a dog. You've read books and have been practicing self-defense with your family. If that's your plan, then you will end up getting killed off before the end of year one, likely after only a few months. Society doesn't exist anymore. The concept of "home" doesn't exist anymore.

But it's still my home, I plan on staying in it!

Only if you can hang on to it. No group of people in history has ever succeeded in withstanding a siege. History is littered with millions of bodies of those that believed they could. From the siege at Masada to the Sieges of Paris and Yorktown, through the Alamo and Stalingrad, time and time again the well-positioned, well-stocked and well-armed defenders always lose. Sooner or later time and circumstance will catch up. Not quite an apples to apples comparison? Maybe so. In that case, if you're looking for the closest thing to a modern-day siege of private homes, residences, compounds, etc. outside of wartime, look no further than Rhodesia.

Modern-day Zimbabwe (another oxymoron) is the tragic, impoverished and economically devastated result of civil war in post-colonial Rhodesia. Much has been written about its ugly birth and childhood, but the essential facts are that Rhodesia was once known as "The Breadbasket of Africa" due to the superior skills and hardiness of the White Farmers, the descendants of British colonial emigrants. They were lured there by the opportunity to set up large, mechanized farms, very cheaply. These farms employed several hundred black locals and provided them food, housing and medical care. 5,000 farms employed almost 1.5 million local black Rhodesians. But no longer. It is now a dead and demolished country. From 1970 through 1979 an intense civil war raged, and open season was declared on the white farmer. Tough though they were, they managed to both farm AND defend their farms while being consistently ravaged and attacked by bands of looters and raiders. Eventually, they succumbed, as all of the other siege victims in history. What makes this story so relevant, however, is that these ridiculously tough, white farmers developed amazingly sophisticated defense mechanisms for their time, including landmines and a radio system. Many articles, survivalist blogs and discussion threads detail these Rhodesian farmers' defensive arrangements. The main point to all of this, of course, *is that they lost. Badly. Many were tortured and killed, women raped, bodies mutilated.* What makes it all worse is that they were brutally defeated by a bunch of completely inept, ignorant, unskilled, ridiculously poor and illiterate vagabonds. It's not like these farmers were up against navy SEALs or Marines or Green Berets. They were defeated by larger numbers of ignorant, savage criminals.

This all happened in a time when the farmers still had water, food, transportation, fuel and rudimentary power. *And they still lost!* Why most survivalists, doomsday bloggers and reality TV shows today would even attempt to promote the same types of security arrangements that those tough, experienced white farmers used *is beyond me.* Especially now in this era of superior small arms and sophisticated long-distance scopes, rifles and hybrid weapons, not to mention night and infrared vision. It all gets back to the same thing. *You can't defend your home if they are coming for it.* Some of you may put up a good fight, but you won't win. History will.

Surely, though, we have better means of defense now-

I won't get into the zombie-like hordes of looters roaming the streets of Sierra Leone and Liberia in the 90's under the brutal regime of Charles Taylor and the ensuing civil war, just yet. I was there, as well. But in South Africa today, the white farmers (otherwise known as Afrikaners) are being subject to the same systematic eradication that happened to the white farmers in Rhodesia. Torture, murder, rape, mutilation, obliteration. Do you think the Afrikaners are oblivious to what happened in Rhodesia? *Of course not!* They thought, in fact, that they had developed "better" defenses! They were ready. *Only they lost, again!* Yes I know the fight still goes on, but really, it's over. Shameful, but again, History repeating itself.

The best defense is a great offense.

Absolutely and unquestionably, which leads us to the point of this entire book: *Offense. You must attack in order to survive. You must become a Raider. A Marauder. A Take-down Champion.* The bulk of remaining humanity will be attempting to become the same thing, of course, but they will not have prepared for it. They will not understand how to do it properly. They will not be ready, and over time most of them will fall, as well. They will attempt to use brute force, which will only work until they come up against more brutal force. *Me.* Maybe you too. Again, History repeats itself, and this is the result.

But what about the Military?

What about it, I guess—As I wrote earlier, it may be good to have an army, but bad that you actually have to feed it. Without the supply chain, those soldiers, airmen, sailors and

Marines will be looking for water and food too. The military will fracture like windshield glass when the supplies run out. Each man will be on his own, and will take his weapons and ammo with him. The Military will disintegrate. That being said, some of those individuals, now acting on their own or in very small groups, will be very formidable indeed. Many of them will be extremely comfortable using rifles, handguns and improvised explosives. Some will have fought for their lives in a foreign country. Many are Special Ops troops. They will stand in the face of fear. They will not hesitate to shoot you. And if they do, you stand a good chance of getting killed— However, the great bulk of ex-Military will not. Why?

Because the great adhesive that holds the Military together is trust and leadership. Both are earned and displayed after training, living and fighting together. If society has fallen, so will this military architecture, rendering many currently in the Military as useless as most of you currently are. Only a select few will band together permanently, or long enough, to succeed.

Only the strong survive.

We CAN learn from the Military, however. Especially when it comes to applying technology to the field of battle. In developing Strategy and Tactics. In improvising explosives. By developing a greater sense of Discipline. By combining this knowledge with lessons learned by the intelligence operations community from the states of anarchy like Liberia and the Balkans, we will build the structure necessary to survive, *even thrive* if the worst ever comes to pass. Only the strong survive, and arising from the ashes of what was civilized human society will be the New Strong, the *Marauders*.

What is a Marauder?

Webster's etymology of the word originates from the French verb *maraud*, describing the intransitive verb *maraudeur*, meaning one roaming about and raiding in search of plunder. I think that describes it very well. In order to survive after the fall of civilized society you will have to roam about in order to locate whatever your specific necessities of life may be, and at some point you may be forced to raid in order to actually obtain them. By definition, now, that makes you a Marauder.

But I don't want to hurt people.

I understand. And you might not have to. But you will certainly have to frighten some of them half to death in order to get what you want from them. This, of course, will be the most difficult thing that the survivors of formerly civilized society will have to come to grips with. The formerly good, caring, conscientious and even God-fearing people will now be faced with the unthinkable in order to enable themselves or their loved ones to survive. Many of us, if we were on our own, might not make that choice. But those of us with a wife or small children will probably not stand by and watch them starve to death—slowly, horribly, painfully.

Whereas before the fall of civilization those good people would "brake for animals," now they might actually have to *kill those animals* to eat, and then kill other humans to defend themselves and their families. Once they do come to grips with it, and kill something for the first time, they might find that it wasn't so terrible after all. They might find that squirrel actually tastes like chicken.

Humans, on the other hand, do not, and will not submit themselves as easily as squirrels. Maybe you won't ever have to kill anybody, but you are easily a fool if you do not become prepared to. I will help you to become prepared. I guarantee it is not as hard as you may think.

OK, so where are we going with this?

Right to the heart of the matter. In order to survive the fall of civilization, it will do you no good to be a hoarder, or a Prepper. *To survive the fall of civilization you will need to become a Marauder.* On the move, attacking first, planning ahead. You will need to develop the mindset of a predator. The rest of this book will guide you in helping to make you successful. You will need to understand handguns and rifles, living in the field, conducting long-term reconnaissance, both night and day, traveling long distances on foot, and above all, acquiring supreme confidence. The confidence that comes with knowing that you are highly trained for the changed and dangerous world that awaits you, more so than 99% of any other humans you may come up against. This confidence, combined with patience, will enable you to acquire anything and everything that you need and/or desire to survive in a post-apocalyptic world. It will enable you to care for your family, your friends, or whoever else you think it is worth risking your life to care for.

This book will challenge those who proclaim the ability to survive an apocalyptic event by using civilized society's principles, and will teach you, the reader, everything that you will need to know, acquire and execute in order to thrive, *yes thrive*, in the event that civilized society, as we know it, comes to an end.

This book will combine real-life instruction with examples from history, and real-life examples from my own experiences in situations where the rule of law had disappeared and where anarchy had reigned. I survived. You can too. I will teach you how.

In the following chapters you will learn about:

- The four most necessary items for survival
- What handguns are really for
- The gun that won the West
- The most dangerous household chemicals
- The value of FLIR
- Night vision scopes
- Explosives
- Moving to where the food is
- Identifying targets of opportunity
- Taking down targets of opportunity
- A dog's real use in the changed world
- Reconnaissance
- Running multiple takedown operations
- Prisoners
- Taking no prisoners

KILKENNY

Among other things. This book is about *action*, not hoarding supplies to last a little while after the fall. Not prepping. You will learn to eat preppers for breakfast. We are happy that they exist, as they are the mom and pop grocery stores of the future. Stores you will happily rob and ravage at will.

CHAPTER 2

Getting Your Game Face On!

Okay, maybe now you have a little bit more realistic idea of what a post-apocalyptic world might feel like. What do you do now?

Forget.

Forget what your everyday life is like today. Forget what you're going to do when you retire. Forget about being around your grandchildren one day (hopefully your kids, if you have any, won't be ignorantly selfish enough to bring new life into the post-apocalyptic hell!). Forget growing comfortably old together with your wife or husband, watching beautiful sunsets, or traveling to Europe, or sitting on the beach in Florida. Just forget all about it.

If you are truly concerned about surviving in the post-apocalyptic world, you need to start moving out of your comfort zone NOW. And I don't only mean physically. It's more important to begin moving out of your psychological comfort zone, and MOST important to begin moving out of your *moral zone* as well. Get uncomfortable, because that is how the post-apocalyptic future will feel. Extremely so. *Get your Game Face on!* How do you begin to do this?

Start breaking the rules.

Again, you're reading this right. To Hell with the rules that will prevent your success after the Fall. Give some serious thought as to what it's going to take to get by in the post-apocalyptic environment. Here's some of my thoughts:

Guns.
Ammo.
Drugs.
Balls.

Simultaneously and interchangeably.

Let's get into this a little bit deeper—Let's start pushing your envelope—you don't live in a state that allows certain types of handguns? Or you need a permit? Or certain weapons are completely banned? Well, *tough shit.* What's more important to you, getting caught 'owning' an illegal weapon, or getting caught with your pants down when the fall of society occurs. I'm not a lawyer (thank God), and I'm not dispensing legal advice, but unless you commit a felony with that weapon nothing is going to happen to you, unless you're stupid enough to drive around with it in your car, and happen to get stopped and searched by the cops. So go out and get what you think works for you (I'll help with that in the next chapter). No matter what type of weapon, illegal or otherwise you own, it's perfectly legal to buy ammo for it, so don't be shy. Go out and get lots of it.

I own three M4's. For the uninitiated, an M4 is the further evolution of the M-16 used in Viet Nam, and is currently the standard issue carbine of the United States Marine Corps. It can fire single shot by single shot, or a burst of three rounds with one trigger pull (my favorite), or go fully machine-gun and unload the magazine by holding down the trigger. It is a very lethal piece of hardware. You've probably also read about the AR-15, which is the civilian version of this weapon. The major differences being it is a semi-automatic, meaning only one round fired with one trigger pull (this is the only mode), and a slightly longer barrel, which make it pretty much like any other pedestrian weapon available to us regular folks. As mentioned above, I own the military version. Fully automatic, fully burned-in by those very same Marines in Afghanistan. If I get caught with them, being in California, that's ten years in the federal pen for me. Do I care? Not one whit. Nothing is going to happen to me. Most cops can't even tell the difference between a fully legal AR-15 and a fully-automatic M4 anyway. Many of them are sympathetic as well. That said, I'm not advocating that you stock up on M4's; actually I think it's a bad weapon to rely on after the Fall if you're not a gunsmith (more later). I'm just telling you that I practice what I preach. In addition, if somebody breaks into my home he's not going to get killed by any of my M-4's. His cause of death will be the Russian Makarov I keep strapped to the back of my nightstand. *A completely illegal handgun in California.* Small, powerful, accurate. A mainstay of the Soviet military for many, many years. So, screw the rules! Go get guns and ammo. As much as you can!

Okay, I'm piling up guns and ammo. Now what?

Start acquiring drugs.

I don't mean coke, heroin or pot. More specifically antibiotics, prescription painkillers, antiseptics and anesthetics, etc. (more on exactly what later on). Start getting aggressive with your doctors—again, let's push your envelope—make up symptoms that can be treated by antibiotics—your doctor will prescribe them, trust me. He might order some tests first, ok big deal. Start going to multiple doctors if necessary. Obamacare will pay for it all! You might also start peeking into the cabinets of your friends and neighbors. You might find what you need in there as well (and you can check the meds by image on the internet). Start hoarding as much medication as possible. Prescription painkillers like Percocet will be more difficult to obtain, but faking lower back pain, or claiming you were in an auto accident, will prompt your doctor to prescribe Vicodin at the very least in the absence of any x-rays or MRI's. Do it often. Take advantage of refills. Pile it all up and store it away. Don't worry about shelf life, either. They last about five times longer than advertised. The drug companies do this to ensure that you keep purchasing them.

Does any of this seem silly or childish to you? If so, then you need an attitude adjustment! You will certainly need these meds at some point after the Fall. What I've suggested above is just a start, of course. You will end up either taking these meds from others or taking out a pharmacy after the Fall. You'll read about that later. What I'm trying to emphasize, of course, is that you need to start somewhere!

I'm thinking by now you get the idea. Change your game plan. Change your thinking. Start changing your mindset from what is legal or what is "right" to *what is right for you!* Forget the rules. Break them if you need to. *Get comfortable with the uncomfortable.* Practice this just for the Hell of it. Things could get a lot worse later on, so taking baby steps now is imperative. You'll never get to the point where you can hold people hostage at gunpoint in order to get what you need to survive if you're completely incapable of lying to your doctor, lifting a few pills from your neighbor's medicine cabinet, or, God Forbid, owning an illegal handgun! Think about it. Hard. This is not a game.

And while you're out practicing anti-establishmentarianism, keep in mind that in order to be successful as a marauder in a post-apocalyptic society you have to, in fact, be physically capable of marauding. That means getting in shape right now. It also means eliminating *right now* potential physical issues that may arise after the fall that may inhibit your ability to go out and get the job done.

What do I mean by this?

Well, do you wear glasses or contacts? Your eyes will only get worse as you age (assuming you do) and there won't be any optometrists around. *Go get Lasik*. Have bad teeth? *Go get voluntary root canal work done*. Have good teeth? *Voluntarily cap and crown all of them*. Sound extreme? Think about a bad cavity, a gum infection or a nerve (root canal) problem and there's no dentist around. *Feeling the pain yet?* Some things you just can't fix on your own. A tooth is one of those things. Forget about acting like Tom Hanks in 'Castaway'. It's actually not that easy to knock a tooth out. Somebody will have to get you really, really drunk, then knock you out cold, then hack away at your tooth until it dislodges, probably in pieces. Then plug or stitch your gum and hope that you have the necessary meds to hold off infection, or at least help your body fight off an infection. *Lots and lots of painkillers.* There's a good chance that this circumstance might end up killing you. I can't think of many things worse (naturally occurring) that could happen to you after the Fall. It might make sense to consider having an oral surgeon as part of your crew-

Which brings us back to drugs.

Infection and pain management will be daily realities in this new environment. One will kill, the other might make you want to kill. Probably yourself! Care to watch your wife, husband or kids suffer from infection or really, really terrible pain? Most of us do not. *So get off your ass and start stockpiling these meds now.* Later on you will learn how to take truckloads from pharmacies or other preppers. But for now this is just a start, enough to get you going, not something to rely on permanently—And while we're on the subject of drugs, keep in mind that you probably should learn when, where and how to use all of them, if you don't know already. Each of us is different, of course, with different issues, so understanding what drugs you may need after the Fall is up to you—So you better figure it out, figure out how to use them, and get working on acquiring them. This will then take you to the next level.

Take a Trauma/Triage class.

These are not your Daddy's first-aid classes you took at boy scouts or even in the military—these were developed for emergency room RN's and PA's. If you don't have any first-aid training at all, then start at your town's community center or local community college and get it done. Then step it up a level. These Trauma/Triage courses are available online. Why is this important? Well, I'm betting that most of you have never actually seen a compound fracture, or somebody's intestines poking out of a deep gash or gunshot wound, or even a good old-fashioned 10 inch laceration tearing a hunk of flesh away. None of this stuff is pretty, or fun. *It's ugly, and deadly.* As a marauder it's likely at some point you'll get lacerated. You might even get a compound fracture. Hopefully you won't get shot. With a deep laceration you or your crew will be alright with time (and Superglue). Same with a compound fracture, assuming it hasn't severed any arteries. If somebody (hopefully not you) has his/her intestines popping out of a gash or bullet hole, well, do the right thing and put a bullet in his/her head. Quickly. That's a hard thing to survive even in today's society, virtually impossible without a surgeon, tons of blood (with a Type match) and meds for sepsis. Uh-uh. It's a slow, ugly painful death. If you care anything at all about that person, then put him down. Immediately.

Which brings us back to attitude.

I'm trying to drive home the point in this chapter that you need to start developing a game face long before an apocalyptic event occurs. There won't be any internet around after the fact to figure out how to do it. I'm hoping you're beginning to understand that you need to start stepping up your game *now!* Then you need to start putting yourself to the test. We've talked about being physically, mentally and morally ready for becoming a marauder. You have guns. You have ammo. You have drugs. You have knowledge. Now you need some experience.

Where do I get some?

Well, shy of becoming a Marine Recon or Navy SEAL, or opting to become a white farmer in South Africa, you're probably not going to experience the real thing. What you can do, though, is put yourself out in a survival situation for a few weeks. By yourself. Get a bush pilot to drop you off in the Alaskan tundra about a hundred miles from base. Make your way back with a map and compass. Carry a rifle and a handgun as you are right in the heart of grizzly and brown bear country. And you're alone. The psychological impact is the hardest, trust me.

What if I get lost?
What if I head the wrong way?
What if I break my leg?
What if a grizzly comes at me?
What if a grizzly takes my food?

Grow some stones, that's what!!

Put yourself out there. You can do it. I know that for many of you it's scary. *It's supposed to be!* That's the point. It will be like that after the Fall; you'll be on your own, you might lose your way, you may have to triage your own injuries, somebody might take your food *and the grizzlies will have guns, which makes them much more dangerous.*

STOP STOP, you say. What about my family?

Okay, you have a family, so you're not quite ready for that just yet—then dial it back a little. Take them on a backpacking trip through a national park for at least a week out on the trail. Preferably in an area with grizzlies. That means Glacier National Park, Banff, Jasper, or pretty much anywhere in Alaska. Bring your weapons. Hopefully you'll see a bear. It will make your trip all the more memorable. Your family might actually enjoy it. These are spectacularly gorgeous places, of course, and there's no better bonding activity than backpacking the wilderness. I'm not going to tell you how to get ready for a trip like that, you can figure that out online or at REI or the North Face Store, where the staffs will be happy to outfit you with everything you need. You will actually use all of this stuff when out marauding, and I will discuss much of this stuff in the next chapter, "The Marauder Toolkit" so consider it money well spent. It beats spending tens of thousands of dollars hoarding.

What you will find throughout the course of the trip is that you are pretty good at some of that stuff, and woefully unprepared for most of it. You will have over-estimated, under-estimated and flat-out just didn't think about a whole lot of stuff. But by the time you're done you will have learned *a lot*. And you've started getting your game face together. What you need to do then is *take more trips*. Bump up the degree of difficulty, boost the number of miles hiked, increase the elevation, worsen the weather conditions. Hike into the heart of the grizzlies. Feel some fear. Understand your response. *Learn, grow, get ready! Again, you can do it!*

And for all of you seasoned backpackers out there, go lose yourself in the wilderness as I mentioned above. Figure out how to navigate without GPS, using only a map, compass, or just by the stars, the topography, or the weather. Put yourself in bear territory. It focuses your senses and forces adaptive behavior. You might actually get attacked and have to shoot one. This, of course, is what you'll need later on.

My son is currently a young Lieutenant in the USMC, and he just completed a training course acronymed SERE, which stands for Survival, Evasion, Resistance, Escape. It was originally designed for pilots and others that might get shot down or lost in enemy territory. It is offered at three levels, A, B and C (C being reserved for Special Ops guys). My son was given level C. It teaches wilderness survival skills, hiding from the enemy, how to get away, and then when you get captured, how to survive your captivity without revealing too much information. It used to be nicknamed "torture school" as up until very recently select students had fun experiencing waterboarding. Supposedly they've done away with that, although they threatened my son's team with it constantly. My son said it was pretty realistic, and after being out alone in the wilderness for five days, then getting the crap beat out of him twice a day for two days, he was getting a little fuzzy. I would say he handled it all admirably up until the point where the "interrogator" (a USMC Sergeant) called him an "Ivy League pussy" as he belted him square in the solar plexus. My son crunched over, of course, but when he straightened back up he head-butted the Sergeant, then cracked him one in the jaw. Down the guy went. Uh-oh, that was a no-no. Then the guy got up! He and my son went at it for a couple of minutes before the whole staff could separate them. *A no-no for both of them*! My son pled 'mental disassociation as a result of the training' and was excused with a reprimand. The Sergeant claimed Self-Defense! They let him off with a reprimand too. No harm, no foul, great for both of them—Anyway, the moral of the story here is that if *you train right, you can do it, and, never, ever, lose your cool.* After the Fall that might spell D-O-O-M.

I took my son on his first backpacking trip when he was 6. He loved it. I taught him navigation when he was 10. He fired his first rifle at 11. He was totally comfortable in the wilderness. I taught him boxing and Hapkido. He was a state champion at full-contact by the time he was 16. The lesson here, again, is that his acquired skill-set helped him glide through SERE. You don't need to actually become a Special Ops guy, but if you train and learn well in anticipation of a Fall, you can make it. *You really can!* However, pay heed to the immortal words of legendary UCLA coach John Wooden:

"Fail to prepare, prepare to fail."

'Nuff said—For any of you interested in learning more about SERE, the first link below is the official one, the second one is a post by graduates.

http://www.marsoc.marines.mil/Units/MarineSpecialOperationsSchool/SERE.aspx

http://www.survivalistboards.com/showthread.php?t=89042

Okay, let's move on again. In addition to everything else discussed here I also highly recommend that you learn to ride. *And I don't mean sitting your ass on the seat of a Harley Fatboy.* Go ride a horse. An honest-to-goodness real-live creature. It will do you good as a continuation of your quest to be out and about in nature too. Horses may well become surviving humanity's primary means of transport again, if the worst happens. They're much easier to take care of than cars, food is readily available, and it's a whole lot easier to steal one. Cars need gas, of course, and someday you'll run out. Or the roads will be clogged with lots of dead cars and other obstacles. Personally I like to fell trees, blocking the paths of vehicles. Cars won't be much good after the first few days, and survivors will sure like to get their hands on them. I myself will consider travelers that I see in cars *"meals on wheels."* Horses can take you out and about at night; cars can't, unless you make yourself a bull's-eye by putting your lights on! Horses are also the ultimate all-weather, all-terrain vehicle. So go learn how to ride one. Don't go out and buy one, of course, as they are expensive as hell to board in today's society. We'll plan on stealing as many as we need when the time comes.

Now it's time for the best way to acquire a really good game face—Weapons Training.

This, of course, is some of the fun stuff. Obviously, if you're ultimately going to be out marauding and raiding after the collapse of civilized society then you better be able to handle guns. Handguns, rifles and shotguns. In the next chapter I will outline and discuss the weapons that I think you need to have in order to be successful. For now, let's just start with getting you comfortable with firearms in general. As with backpacking gear, I'm not going to show you how to do this. It would take up the whole book and that's not the point. The best way to learn and get comfortable is by personal, one on one instruction, preferably by somebody who's actually used a rifle or handgun in a combat situation. If you have any buddies who've been in combat go pay them to teach you everything they can. If they're not available go out and find a Marine or Army Infantryman. Any Marine will do, as they are all riflemen first. If you don't know any military, then go online and find a weapons training course near you. Go watch, check references, etc. Many of them are really, really good, but not necessarily cheap. Ammo can be expensive too, but it's a necessary cost. If you have a family, get them indoctrinated as well. They're going to have to help you at some point, and if they can't shoot somebody when you need them to then you might as well shoot *them*—then yourself.

Let's pause here for a moment.

Don't get too far ahead of yourself here. Unless you're already ex-military, Intelligence, or a cop in the Bronx you're never going to reach the skill level of any one of them. So don't get carried away thinking all of a sudden you're a badass 'cause you've got all this weapons training. *That will get you killed quicker than shit.* Watch an episode of "Doomsday Preppers." All of these idiots learn how to shoot handguns. The problem is they're slow, they can't hit anything, and they look so horribly uncomfortable (and ridiculous) using them. That's good news for you, as they are sheep on the way to slaughter. They hope that they will never, ever have to even grab a weapon; you, on the other hand, hope to be drawing one every day. You will become better with time. More comfortable, more accurate. CAUTION—you don't want to get in a straight-up shoot out with ex-Navy SEALS or Marines. You'll stop breathing out of that hole in your forehead before you can squeeze a shot off.

Fortunately, this is not part of the plan. We will seek to avoid straight-up firefights, even though you would win 99% of them. As you will learn later on in Marauding 101, your primary weapon will be psychological. But for now remember who you are and what your limitations may be. Learning how to handle weapons and how to shoot is great. You might even get really good at hitting fixed targets. But as Bruce Lee famously commented about board-breaking stunts, *"Boards don't hit back."* Well put. I think that sums it up nicely.

CHAPTER 3

The Girl from Ipanema

The story that follows may shed a little light on how my style came to develop over time. It also highlights that your own little world can go to Hell in a heartbeat—How you react when it does, and how you are prepared to deal with it, is what this book is about. This little story from my past should help to serve as an example. We'll break it down at the end-

Sometime in the late 80's early 90's I was doing quite a bit of commercial business in Mexico, and in particular I was doing quite a bit of transportation company financing. I was working with both Aeromexico and Mexicana, the railroads, shipping lines, trucking companies, everybody. The granddaddy of them all was Mexico Transport. I had developed very deep relationships with Mexico Transport's president and his financial management team. The relationship got remarkably deeper by accident one day, as the Chairman, Alejandro Navarro, called my home in the U.S. unexpectedly while I was on the road (ostensibly to beat me up over the provisions in some Transportation leases). My wife (the former hot Colombian girlfriend) answered the phone and when he asked to speak with me she politely asked him to hold a second, and then promptly unleashed a tirade of invective upon my three kids, in Spanish! Intrigued, Alejandro began speaking to her in Spanish, inquired as to her background, and they became fast friends. My wife and I had dinner with him quite often in Mexico and the US after that.

Okay so what?

Well, my coziness with Mexico Transport's Chairman, of course, caught the attention of certain U.S. interests. These interests suspected that some financial foul play might be occurring at MT, and that some "important" U.S. investors might get hurt. U.S. Intelligence asked me to investigate; to sniff out what was going on and try to get in on the action, whatever that was. I said ok, for the right price.

Getting My Game Face On

Well, turns out that MT's intelligence was better than ours at that point, as they certainly were expecting someone like me to come looking. I went down to Mexico City from Toronto using my Canadian Passport and identity (I looked something like Ben Affleck in Argo. Pretty bad but a good disguise). I arrived Mexico City and promptly caught a cab to the Nikko Hotel. Took off my Argo wig and beard, put on a Hugo Boss charcoal-gray suit, white shirt, burgundy tie and walked a ways over to the Hotel Marquis, then checked in there under my U.S. identity and passport. Emptied some liquor bottles, ran the shower, messed up the bed. Left the hotel in a taxi bound for the hotel Radisson. In the Radisson's lobby bathroom I changed back to Ben Affleck and walked back to the Nikko. It was a beautiful, warm summer night.

I had dinner at the bar, ordered a few drinks, hit on the pretty little Mexican waitresses. I made myself very visible. One of the waitresses actually agreed to hook up with me when she got off work! Too bad I would be starting work then! I left the hotel about 11 pm and walked over to MT's offices, located conveniently on the Paseo de la Reforma, right next door to the Hotel Marquis.

Here We Go!!

Security consisted of a "guard" who made you sign in. Only the employees were allowed access to the building after 9pm, so I showed my fake Mexico Transport "Finanzas" ID which verified me as an employee in the finance department, ostensibly going upstairs to finish a report for the Chairman in the morning. I pushed the "up" button next to the tiny elevator door. *Whew, that was easy.* I got off at the sixth floor, which led to the Finance Department, then hiked up the backstairs to the top floor, where Alejandro's office was. I was starting to sweat a little bit now—not only because of the absence of AC in the stairwell, but also because of the cameras that were moving around in there. I was banking on the hope that Jose' down in the lobby wasn't watching them, as he had been watching Futbol' on the little TV in front of him when I walked in. The security monitors were behind him. I had also hit the down button on the elevator so it was opening up on his floor right about now-

Onto the top floor. Quiet and dark. A little too dark, which made me a little uncomfortable. These idiots usually never flip a light switch. Never mind though. Alejandro's was the only office door that was completely solid, while all of the others throughout the building had a glass-patterned pane half way up. This was in the days before magnetic card swiping, so his office door lock, *Hecho en Mexico,* was a cinch to pick. No visible alarm. Inside I could see with my penlight his immaculate office, as it always was. I knew, though, that through Alejandro's closet and on the other side was another office. I figured that was where he took his secretaries, until now. *That's where the pot of gold is.* I picked both locks again, and entered his tiny little hidden office on the other side of the closet. As I closed the door I turned and was promptly clocked in the jaw by one of the biggest Mexican guys I'd ever seen. *Really, they're not a large people!* Before I could get up he and another guy had me pinned and were putting the cuffs on, behind my back. Not much I could do. I spoke to them only in English, pretending not to know Spanish, hoping they might be stupid enough to speak to each other in Spanish. They were.

Could have used the Marauder toolkit.

Curiously enough, we headed toward the back staircase. Not a good sign. Then the little guy spoke up in Spanish asking the big guy what he thought "they" might do with me. "No se, pero no yo creo que nadie jamas' lo volveria a ver" he answered, laughing. Loosely translated it means 'nobody's gonna see THIS dude again.' I started laughing too, although my jaw hurt really bad and I now had pain in one of my molars. We exited out below the ground floor, then up and outside through a narrow and not very tall dimly lit staircase by the trash bins. There was a Mexican Police cruiser parked there, waiting. *Crap.*

Now, I know what you're thinking. "Mexican Police" is another oxymoron, as, well, they're just morons. Happened to be true in this case as well. The little guy opened the rear door as the bigger one shoved me face down, hard, onto the rear floor. *Asshole.* I think my jaw is broken. I heard him say "Gracias Enrique, El Patron es en dueda contigo." Thanks Henry, the big guy owes you one. I know what this means. Alejandro is, in fact, dirty. Very dirty. He knew somebody like me was coming, and wanted whoever sent me to think twice about sending another, given what they were going to do to me. I don't think he was thinking it was US intelligence though—*Not that it would help ME in my current situation.* A bigger problem for Alejandro down the road.

Now, these are not the Mexican Police that exist today. This is before the Federal Police were created in 1999 due to all of the local corruption throughout Mexico (which still exists today anyway). This was some unit of the Auxiliary Police, similar to the smaller Metropolitan Police Force operating under a big city PD, something like that. They have dozens of little local police "stations" scattered around Mexico City. The one they took me to was in a typical Mexico City neighborhood located outside the Zona Rosa, or Tourist Zone, which means dark and shitty! It had dual bullet-resistant glass front doors, a backlit, rectangular white lightbulb sign that read "SSP" and nothing else on the exterior. It was made of painted white cinderblock. Inside the dual doors is a wall with a metal door and a separate bullet-resistant window. Two crappy wood chairs off to one side. It reminded me of the entrance to the police station in L.A. where they held Sarah Connor in "The Terminator," in which Arnold utters his immortal line, *"I'll be back."* I am not Arnold, however, and am not feeling so confident. I'm not sure I'll be back either, as I've stumbled onto something big, and it doesn't feel like it's going to end well.

This is why you need to practice! Shit Happens.

'Enrique' opens the back door of the cruiser and drags me out. He looks like Sgt. Schultz from Hogan's Heroes, save the black hair and black moustache. *Classic!* An electronic buzz that sounds like a dying bumblebee lets us through the glass doors to the station and then a second, weaker buzz lets us through the large metal door into the station. Four old-style metal desks. Gray. Papers piled up all over them spilling onto the floor. Crap everywhere. Paper bags, plastic bags, police duct tape, just shit. The walls are a dingy light gray about 5 feet up, then a dingy white the rest of the way up to the drop ceiling covered sporadically with those crap acoustic tiles. All poorly lit by some old-fashioned fluorescent 4' tubes. What a dump! This whole area is about 35' square. A younger-looking Mexican cop is sitting at the closest desk to the entry door, obviously the guy who let us in. He chats up Enrique and says that "Gordo" is in the back. I think his name is Hector. Along the back wall are two rectangular windows, and another solid metal door. That's where we're headed.

Through the door and on the other side are two larger wooden desks, and two small jail cells. File cabinets line the far back wall, about 5' tall running the length of the wall to the cells.

Same wonderful color and decorating scheme. This room totals about 25x12. Gordo is definitely there, waiting. Gordo is, in fact, gordo. Muy gordo! Hugely fat, greasy, scummy. Every stereotype you can apply to corrupt Mexican cops is on display around his taco sweat-stained bulging waistline. He makes Sgt. Schultz look small. The only interesting thing about this sweaty pig is that he has two pearl-handled Colt .45 revolvers strapped to that 80" belt around his waist. Wonder where he got those . . .

It's just then that I notice for the first time, huddled in the fetal position in a corner of the front cell, an absolutely stunning Mexican girl, great makeup, pearl earrings, longish-sky blue silk dress, a hint of red in her long, wavy silky hair. Greenish eyes. Perfectly coiffed, really gorgeous, and crying. Sobbing really. I've been around Latin America long enough to know that she is a very, very high-priced prostitute. Government clientele. She would normally never ever see the inside of a place like this. She must have really pissed off some corrupt government official who probably tried to stiff her or something. Again, *Shit Happens!*

Momentarily, my thoughts shifted away from my own hairy predicament and over towards hers. I can guess what's going to happen to her, but there's not much I can do about that either. Weird that we're both in the same place though. Or not-

Gordo's real name is Gonzalo, and he tells Sgt. Schultz to lock me in the other cell, and tells Hector in front to go get dinner. And take his time. Interestingly, he removes my cuffs before shoving my face into the bars on the far side of the cell. *Asshole!*

KILKENNY

No Joke my face is killing me. Door slides and clangs behind me. "The sound of inevitability." There's nothing to sit on. No bunk, chair or toilet. Clearly a holding cell where they are going to prepare me for my journey to the afterlife.

"You're lucky amigo" Gordo says to me in pretty good English. He's clearly the boss. "You have one more hour left here then you go. But now you watch the show!" Smiling, laughing and clearly proud of himself, he is a complete moron. He just gave me all the information I needed, without even asking. I now know that some other team is coming to get me in about an hour, and it will probably end in my death as he's gonna rape this babe and make me watch. He doesn't care about me as he knows there's not gonna be a witness. Now I have to go for broke. No standing before a judge for me in the morning.

So that fat greasy pig slides open the door to her cell slowly, letting the obnoxious squeak grate on my already highly-strung nerves. Probably on hers too. She gets up and starts yelling at him, not in fear, but angrily. In really bad Spanish! Then I pick out a phrase "Que le Cuse!" which roughly translated means 'what the fuck is your problem'. Only it's not Spanish, it's Portuguese—This hot babe is Brazilian! I knew there couldn't be a Mexican girl that gorgeous—Anyway, he moves in as she moves away to the other corner, really nowhere to go. He closes the gap like a cat and cracks her in the face, but she up and knee-smashes him in the balls! He grunts but yanks an 8" inch stiletto from his enormous waistband and slices her left cheek; then holds it there, pressing it with all his 500 pounds against her lovely face, the point resting right on the edge of her left eye. *What a fucking dick!* The wound was almost bloodless, as this was the old fashioned, one-piece supersharp blade they carried in the old days, each edge honed to infinite perfection. A beautiful weapon, just horribly used on a beautiful woman.

I knew at that moment I would kill Gordo if I got out of this. She's now deadly silent as he slams her on the floor, reaches up under that beautiful silk dress and tears her panties off. That fucking pig sniffs them long and hard and sticks them in his back pocket. *A souvenir. He's done this before.* My anger is reaching all-time high levels. The stiletto now slices like butter from the bottom of her dress all the way up to and through the round neck at the top. He slices the pearl necklace off her neck and it spills all over the shitty sticky floor. He lays open her dress for all of us to see. "Bella, no?" he says to us. As she lay there in silence I am reminded of Jesus Christ, head tilted down sideways, blood droplets running down her cheek and down her chest between her large beautiful breasts, arms held straight out to her sides, legs tight together and straight down, bent slightly at the knees. It's hard for me today to look upon a statue of Christ without seeing her on the cross instead.

She does not resist. The fight is gone. Fatboy drops his humongous pants, tugs on his tiny cock a little, and right before he drops on her I yell "Wait, wait, when you're done don't kill her, I want to fuck her too! I know I'm dead anyway so maybe you can just give me one last time! I'll give you the code to my ATM and I'll tell you where I hid cash in my room at the Nikko Hotel. Two grand. Please! You have my passport and key. If I leave my scum in her you can hang this on me too, then maybe you won't have to kill her!" She won't squeal if she lives."

Gordo laughs a big jelly belly laugh, and because of his huge ego and arrogance, actually agrees! Again this goes back to the "moron" part of "oxymoron." I leap up and yell "yesyesyes thank you gracias take my cash I can't wait to fuck her!! Hurry up!! I'm up at the bars watching, and now Fatass drops on top of this beautiful young girl and starts to brutally rape her, smacking her without cause every minute or so, just for the fuck of it. *He is clearly a psychopath.* She grunts with every hard shove, but I think more from that asshole's bulk than from the act itself. "Smack!!" again "Smack!! Again. "Don't fuck up her face!!" I yell. I want her to suck on it! I'm up at the gate opening my pants telling Enrique "Hurry man open it up I'm gonna pop!" Sgt. Schultz comes over as Gordo is clearly orgasming, I'm jumping up and down on my toes with anticipation, opening my pants, Enrique says "espera espera" and he comes over to open the door to my cell as Fatass utters his last grunt. I'm outside staring into her cell and she is staring back at me like "Jesus Christ will dismember you piece by piece and feed you to Satan!" Sgt. Shultz opens her cell door and I SLAM AROUND LIKE MICKEY MANTLE BATTING LEFTY AND FROM HIPS TO SHOULDERS DRIVE MY RIGHT ELBOW INTO ENRIQUE'S THROAT I FEEL THE CRUNCH AND HE DROPS LIKE SONNY LISTON I THINK HE'S DEAD GORDO TRIES TO GET UP BUT MISS BRAZIL LOCKS HER THIGHS AROUND HIM AS HE AGAIN CRACKS HER IN THE FACE GIVING ME ENOUGH TIME TO DROP ON GORDO AND START STRANGLING HIM WITH MY BELT I PULL HIM BACK UP ON HIS ASS FROM BEHIND ON TOP OF ME AS HE STRUGGLES I YELL TO HER "CUCHILLO!" AND SHE GRABS THE STILETTO I NOD DOWN TO THE LEFT AND

SHE GETS IT SWINGING HARD AND FAST AND SLICING OFF GORDO'S COCK IN ONE MOVE THEN STUFFING IT IN HIS MOUTH AS HE'S CHOKING I LET HIM TASTE HIS OWN COCK FOR A MINUTE BEFORE I APPLY THE CRUNCHING BLOW AND KILL THAT MOTHERFUCKER AS I SAID I WOULD.

Sgt. Schultze is on his back gasping for breath, holding his throat. I walk over, lift him up, roll him gently onto my lap and tell him "esta bien, esta bien" it's ok, it's ok, then I hold his head close to my chest and SNAP hmmph HIS hmmph FUCKING hmmph NECK.

It turns out her name was Natalia, and she had just arrived in Mexico the day before. Hector is still out at dinner, or out banging his mistress like all other Mexican cops do on Saturday night before they go to Church on Sunday morning with their wives and kids. I collect Fatass' Beautiful pearl-handled pistols (my souvenir) and the stiletto, and head out. We walk about a mile before we can find a cab, and I offer him $50 U.S. to drop us two blocks from the only safe house address I have. It's out by the airport. When we arrive he asks for $50 more. I laugh and say no thanks I'm out of cash, but this retard won't let it go. He turns facing me and pulls a 40-year old snub .38. *Asshole! Clearly I am in NO FUCKING MOOD so I put a pearl-handled .45 round through his left ear, out the right ear and smashing out the driver window. Then I drive his taxi with the window down to the*

Zona Rosa, dump it on a back street and catch another taxi back to the safe house.

Some of you may have seen the movie "Safe House" with Denzel Washington. It's a really cool, high tech, totally secure modern facility with every cool gadget you can think of. Well, not the case here. I don't know if things have changed that much in 30 years, or if they just gave me the shitty places. I've only been in two safe houses my whole life. This was my first. It was in the back of an auto repair shop on a dingy side street in one of Mexico City's worst neighborhoods. When I showed up asking for Uncle Sam they knew who I was already and had quarters set up. They were not expecting the girl, but set something up for her as well. It had a couple of dingy bedrooms and a living room, a kitchen, and satellite TV. Anything I wanted, though, the guys working the safe house could get, no questions asked. They arranged communication for me and suffice to say I called a full strike on Mexico Transport's offices, told them where to go, and to go get Alejandro Navarro. Net net, a combined U.S. Mexican team collected everything, and went after Alejandro. He promptly absconded to Switzerland with $120 million. Mexico got most of it back; But Alejandro never did any real time. Convicted three times, his sentences were suspended. That's where the rest of his $120 million went, I guess. At least he didn't profit from it. *I guess you could call that a success.* And the fact that there were now two less psycho Mexican cops around, a world better with them gone.

Natalia recovered well. She clung pretty tight to me for a couple of days. *I didn't mind.* The guys at the safe house got her a new identity and a new Brazilian passport. I had the guys from the safe house retrieve my stuff from the Hotel Marquis, and I adopted my U.S. identity again, surrendering Ben Affleck and the beard. She and I flew to Brazil, spent a couple of days in the Cesar Park Hotel on Ipanema beach decompressing before I set her up in a pretty good job as an admin for Petrobras (the Brazilian state-owned oil company). A few years later she married an American businessman I had introduced her to, and they now live happily in a big U.S. city with two teenage boys. I see her quite frequently, and she, of, course, has never forgotten what I did for her. Some horror stories do have happy endings.

Did you feel any of that? Did any of it make you sick? How about that brutal rape or me killing three lowlifes? Any of you think *I'm* the asshole?

Well I hope on some level that you were affected in some way. Obviously I think about it often. I learned early on that the world is a horribly dangerous and mostly random place. My little story was meant to highlight three sure-fire situations that will develop after the Fall:

One—there will be some idiots out there that will acquire enough power to make themselves believe they can proclaim themselves "The Law."

Two—many, many women will get raped. Many, many times.

No way, you say-

But why? *This is the history of Mankind.* As I said in an earlier chapter, History always wins. Just for fun, let's examine events that have occurred recently, as in the late 20th century until now. The chart below is courtesy of the Christian Science Monitor. No editing, a direct cut and paste-

Rape during recent wars and civil unrests:

- More than 20,000 Muslim girls and women were raped during the religiously-motivated atrocities in the former Yugoslavia in Bosnia. This was mainly during an organized Serbian program of cultural genocide. One goal was to make the women pregnant, and raising their children as Serbs. [1] Another was to terrorize women so that they would flee from their land.
- It has been estimated that Iraqi soldiers raped at least 5,000 Kuwaiti women during Iraq's invasion of Kuwait. [2]
- During the civil war in Rwanda: *"One United Nations report estimated that as many as 500,000 women and girls suffered brutal forms of sexual violence, including gang-rape and sexual mutilation, after which many of them were killed."* [3]
- According to a UNESCO article: *"In Algeria, the women of entire villages have been raped and killed. The government estimates that about 1,600 girls and young women have been kidnapped to become sexual slaves by roving bands from armed Islamic groups."* [2]

This of course is not addressing here the aftermath of Natural Disasters, like the most recent decimation of Haiti after the recent earthquake. It is estimated that in the refugee camps there over a hundred thousand women have been raped, and are continuing to be. And sadly, lastly, let's not forget the #1 Rape Land of all time, *Liberia*. Over 90% of the women alive today in that lawless shithole have been raped. 80% have been raped multiple times! *That would be millions and millions of rapes!* And these are places that the UN actually "patrols"!!

Listen everyone, it's the 21st century and this problem is as bad as it ever was. When there is no law, or fear of any existing law, men rape women. Brutally. It's a fact. Some of us do not, of course, but you can bet your ass it will be rampant in a post-apocalyptic society.

Look, I don't want to dwell on this too much longer, but think about all of the different situations that will lead to this—criminal gangs, men who declare themselves law, young men with no wives or girlfriends, no social structure for meeting women and developing a normal male/female relationship, the unmarried men in your Doomsday Prepper colony who after only a few months will get sick and tired of being around other men with wives or girlfriends having sex and will start taking them as well. The scenarios are endless . . .

So unless these post-apocalyptic women are like Milla Jovovich in "Resident Evil" or Michelle Rodriguez in, well, anything, a whole lot of time and effort also needs to be put forth to protect any woman important enough to you. This will probably involve attachment of explosives to them for self-detonation. MAD. Mutually Assured Destruction. It might work better than a chastity belt-

As for those who lay claim to laying down the law, they should be killed instantly. You're not going to make many, if any, friends in this new world. Somebody says they make the rules, kill them right then and there, because what they really mean is that they will do what they want with you.

But Kilkenny, what if I run across the one group that actually might be friendly and I've killed them?

Well, *Shit Happens! You can't trust anybody. See what you just did to the 'friendly' people?!*

Ok, I didn't spell out the third sure-fire thing that is bound to occur after the fall:

Three—you will reach a point where you just say "Fuck it!" and you will act, maybe almost suicidally, but you will. I first reached that point *before* Gordo started raping that beautiful Brazilian girl. You should reach that point as well. If you don't, well, then you're a useless piece of shit-

> ***"One Man With Courage Is A Majority"***
> **—Thomas Jefferson, June 1776**

CHAPTER 4

The Marauder Toolkit

Okay now let's talk about what we really need to get going—*The Marauder Toolkit*. It's much like a 'bag of tricks' consisting of many items, broken down primarily into two categories: Equipment and Supplies. The well—equipped Marauder will have all of the following:

EQUIPMENT

>   Handguns
>   Rifles
>   Shotguns
>   Lots of Ammo
>   Binoculars
>   Night Vision
>   Heat Vision
>   Body Armor
>   Tear Gas
>   Backpacking Equipment
>   Hunting Knives
>   Portable Water Filters
>   Mini-Solar Battery Rechargers

A Horse
Dogs. Three or four
A Couple Of Secure Locations To Store All This Crap
Balls. Big Ones.

SUPPLIES

Triage Kit
Gasoline
Handyman Toolbox
Lots of Empty Wine and Beer Bottles
Piano Wire
Bleach
Ammonia
Oven Cleaner
Lighters
Matches
Road Flares

I'm going to treat some of these categories as mini-chapters, so don't be confused by the blank page. It Has Been Intentionally Left Blank. Some of these categories I will group together, like "Ammonia" and "Bleach," and some of these categories I will ignore, for example the "Handyman Toolbox." If you don't know what a toolbox is then tell whoever is reading this book to you to stop and help you go potty.

Okay, let's start with the obvious—

HANDGUNS

So now you've got some experience handling weapons, and you've figured out how ridiculously hard it is to hit anything with a handgun out past 20 feet without taking too much time aiming at it. That, of course, is not good because I can close a 20-foot gap between you and me in about 1 second. That doesn't leave you much time to shoot me if you need to, and I won't be closing that gap to ask if you're having a nice day!

Okay, so what good are handguns?

Not much, really, if you intend to use them to take stuff from other people. Handguns are better for up close and personal last-ditch self-defense, as they're obviously much, much more maneuverable in tight quarters than rifles or shotguns. They're also pretty useful in situations where you've already got the drop on somebody. Or for target practice. A highly decorated Marine Corps veteran once wrote that a handgun is really great for holding out until you can get back to your rifle— Which you should never have left in the first place. What's really needed here to do a good job at marauding is a good long gun. But we'll get to that in a little bit. For now-

So many guns, so little time-

First let me say that I'm not trying to write a technical treatise on ballistic weapons. Just the basics, to reaffirm for the Faithful and to indoctrinate the Uninitiated. *If you're a know-it-all then skip these sections.* If you want to learn something, or are just curious, read on. I've actually got some experience using these things for real.

Handguns—like golf clubs, tennis rackets, running shoes, or baseball bats—are really a matter of personal choice. They all need to meet a certain standard of course, but once they do, the rest is about their primary use, reliability, competence at the task and ease of use. Try asking 10 different experienced handgun owners and shooters what "the best" handgun out there is. You'll get ten different answers. Combat veterans with heavy handgun experience have a slightly different take, as usually they've been forced to use a single type of sidearm, and like most other things they've owned and used over a long period of time, they highlight the flaws. Even if a handgun has excellent characteristics in every category, some Navy SEAL will tell you about the time his Sig 226 jammed right as he had the defining shot, and if he had the chance he would toss that piece of shit overboard and get a Glock 17 (just an example). For me, this discussion gets old and boring, and I'm sure it will for you all as well. You can go online and type in "ten best handguns" or "most accurate handguns" even "most reliable" and "best of all time" and you won't get any kind of consensus. But I encourage you to do so in order to get some understanding of what others have experienced with all of these individual weapons.

One thing you probably *will* find majority support for, maybe even a consensus in some places, is a handgun's *caliber*. For the uninitiated, this is the diameter of the bullet (or barrel) used in that handgun. It is generally measured in tenths of an inch, as in the "22" (.22 inches) or the "45" (.45 inches, etc.). Simply put, these are the diameters of the barrel of that weapon and the bullet fired through it. Some weapons are referenced by their measurement in millimeters, such as the "9-millimeter," or 9mm. The .357 and the 9mm have identical measurements. The exception to this rule of relationship to size and name is the old "38," as it is also the same caliber as the .357 and the 9mm (why, I don't know but I'm sure one of you out there does and will let the rest of us in on it). The size that most handgun owners prefer is the 9-millimeter.

Why?

Stopping Power, i.e. the ability to stop an assailant coming at you or firing at you, with only one or two shots (as you might miss 4 or 5 shots). Since a .22 round is small, it requires a small charge to jar it loose from its casing, propel it down the barrel and bury it into the flesh of your victim. A .45 is pretty darn big by comparison, and needs a proportionately bigger charge to dislodge the bullet, get it out of the gun and into your target. The side effect to this, of course, is the amount of power it has left when it reaches the target. *A lot*. Therefore it will "stop" the intended victim quite easily. The .45 also has plenty of "recoil," the force that makes the gun almost jump out of your hands when you shoot it, making it harder to hit anything with.

Recoil is a problem for many shooters, and therefore gives rise to the other school of thought regarding caliber, "Placement." This is the ability to more easily and effectively hit your victim, in more potentially deadly places, using a weapon with low recoil and thereby offering a better "shot placement." Using a lower caliber weapon to reduce or eliminate recoil in order to better place a bullet into a softer target—like an eyeball, or throat, bare lower abdomen, etc.

So how do we decide?

Well, again, this book isn't supposed to be a technical work on weapons; you can find enough of that stuff online if you have trouble sleeping at night. All you really need to know is that neither approach is better than the other. Everything depends on you, *the shooter*, and how good/fast/seasoned courageous you are. Now, I know I'll get a ton of mail from the 9mm crowd calling me an idiot and hoping I run into a guy some moonless night on a wet backstreet pointing a 9mm at me while I'm holding a BB gun. Then I should be able to get great shot placement with all my 15 BB's until I get knocked into next week by a single 9mm round to my breastbone. Well, I'll bet that most of those mail-writers have never been in a straight-up shootout with a handgun before. As I referenced earlier, "Boards don't hit back" (from Bruce Lee). Neither do paper range targets. For those who have been in a few scrapes (primarily Military and Police), you probably had 9mm's or 38's and can bark at me all you like and I won't bark back. You've earned the right. As for the rest of you, well-

So what do I prefer and what will I use?

Both.

That's not a chicken-shit answer, either. In terms of fun, hitting the range, or targets way out in the field, I'm a big fan of a big gun. *The 1911*. Google it. *The* classic American handgun. It's a .45 caliber, big and heavy, all-steel. A man's gun. Moderate recoil for that large a charge. Immaculately accurate. I can hit anything with it at any reasonable distance, if I have enough time to aim it. And because it's a big, heavy, long gun, you actually have to aim it. If all I've got is this weapon and trouble is 50 yards out, I start shooting, they go down, no worries-

That said, there's a 'lighter' side to my handgun preferences, the Makarov, in 9mm (roughly), and the CZ-83 and the cold-war era Walther PP, both in .32 caliber.

The .32 caliber is just about halfway between the .22 and the .45. There are quite a few newer designs and plenty of other manufacturers around, but they now all have a large plastic component in their product (polymer, I know I know, but it's still, well, plastic), which directly affects durability and recoil. The Walther PPK, as many of you already know, was James Bond's gun in the Sean Connery series of films. The old-school Walther is easy to carry and conceal, is solid enough, all steel, and has enough weight to make the recoil of the .32 caliber charge disappear, which makes it a really soft shooter. One of the best gun designs ever, extremely accurate. I can fire both the CZ and the Walther with one hand, and actually hit stuff. That's actually pretty hard to do outside of Hollywood. The CZ is a Czech-made Military/Police weapon, very similar to the Walther in design, style, size and weight. A better shooter in my experience. I can get great shot placement in a short period of time with both of these guns, and trust me, you take a round from one and you stop. Don't believe any of that bullshit you read about a guy not knowing he's been hit by a .32 during a firefight. He knows, and if he's still on his feet it will alter his thinking. That's all you'll need.

These old .32's are two of the most reliable handguns, of any caliber, out there. Reliability, of course, being extremely important *when you actually have to rely on them.* Guns jam. Springs fail. Magazines crack. Lead builds. *Shit happens!* That's all expected, of course. Which is why we take good care of our weapons.

In case any of you care, my favorite weapon is the Russian Makarov. It fires a bullet a little bit wider than a 9mm, (9.2mm) and a little bit shorter. Basically a stubbier 9mm round. Another Cold War weapon. Why is it my favorite weapon? Like the Walther and the CZ, and based on the Walther design, it is compact, all steel, heavy, minimizes recoil, is extremely accurate, and never fails. *Never.* I've never had a jam. You could load gravel through that thing. That's why I keep it strapped to my nightstand. Somebody gets past my bedroom door I know I can empty the magazine. No Jams. Total Peace of Mind.

So where does this leave us?

My suggestion is to carry a long handgun (the 1911 let's say) with great range and heavy firepower, and also a compact, solid steel gun you can empty quickly in close quarters with one hand. One caveat here: in the last year or so the 1911 has gotten completely out of control in terms of price. And in a similar fashion to the AR-15, the newer models really require a huge amount of maintenance over time. So I will offer an alternative, one I own as well. The CZ-75B. Probably a better all-around gun, little maintenance, and about a third of the cost of a 1911. Call CZ-USA if you need more info. Pretty much the same gun in terms of size, weight and performance. It's just not made in the U.S.! For women, I think a .22 will work just fine. No recoil, low noise factor. It can be quickly emptied. Put three or four .22 rounds out of fifteen into a guy and he's going down, if you actually have the time to get the shots off. That's the trade-off, of course. Placement vs. Stopping Power, and how you deal with it is your own choice.

What about Ammo?

Well, ammo also opens up great debate and disagreement among the throngs of the gun-owning faithful. The good news, however, is that 9mm and .45 ammo grow on trees. Expensive trees, but they're everywhere. 9x18 (Makarov) ammo is plentiful as well, but also more expensive. .32 caliber ammo is probably the toughest to get, and probably the most expensive at this point. In a post apocalyptic environment we will be stealing ammo, more likely than not it will be .45, 9mm and .22, so spend your money *today* on the .32, assuming you choose to use that weapon. I already have enough Mak ammo.

Before we move on, I think it's a good idea to suggest that you pay no attention to loads, foot pounds of pressure, full metal jacket, hollow points, all that technical garbage relating to the type of round to use. As I mentioned before, any .45, 9mm, or .32 round will kill your enemy (though it might take three or more 22's). What we will have in the next life is what we find, or what we take. If the box says 9mm, or .45 or .32 or 9x18, it will load and it will kill.

Lastly, maintenance and cleaning, as with most machines, is the key to long, reliable use. Learn how to take apart your weapon and put it back together. Learn how to clean it properly. Buy extra mags, springs, other parts. Learn how to replace springs or slides or whatever a non-gunsmith can do. It's actually pretty easy stuff, but all of it is unique to the handguns you end up purchasing. Your livelihood will depend on it.

RIFLES

Well, here we go again. As with handguns, there is no consensus at all as to which rifle is the best. There are many more options for caliber and configurations. No agreement or consensus regarding their caliber, barrel length, distance capability, dependability, weight, scopes, magazine capacity, ammo *OH MY GOD* it goes on and on . . .

Like handguns, ask 10 experienced shooters to name the best rifle and you get 10 different answers. And rightly so in this case. There's a lot more to consider when choosing a rifle. Nowadays they come in all shapes, sizes, materials, calibers and even colors. *They sell pink rifles for Christ's sake!* For any single caliber you can get different barrel lengths, long range capability, short range capability, iron sights or scopes, high capacity mags, low capacity mags, fully automatic, semi-automatic or burst. Waterproof. Dirtproof. Bugproof, etc. etc. etc . . . And if you happen to agree with any one of the ten people you ask, the other nine will think you are a child using your mommy's computer or just a plain and simple idiot. Period.

One of the best articles I've read about this debate was posted on the "End of Days No Days Off" gun blog. Visit their site for the full article:

http://www.everydaynodaysoff.com/2009/12/30/pros-and-cons-of-possible-shtf-rifle-choices/

Captures it perfectly! Highly entertaining! Some of the highlights, courtesy of ENDO, below-

The AR 15:
Great, awesome, unbelievable rifle (when it works). Can hit a fly in the ass at 300 yards (when it works). If one is ever attacked by a pack of feral poodles post-SHTF, this is the perfect defensive rifle (unless it jams, in which case you're poodle food). The upside is that one can hang more plastic aftermarket doo-dads on it than a Christmas tree, which may effectively frighten away bad guys when the gun jams.

The MINI-14:
Could be a good rifle, but it's not black.

The SKS:
Best obsolete rifle ever made (even if it isn't black). If lying in a big mud puddle and shooting bad guys, this is the rifle to have. It shoots best when full of mud, and the ten round mag makes puddle shooting a breeze as you can hold the rifle upright in prone (mud puddle) position. Major drawback is that in a

post-SHTF situation one must constantly fire thousands of rounds, a task for which the fixed ten round magazine is ill equipped (that's why they invented the AK). The aftermarket hi-capacity mags often jam, creating the illusion that one is shooting an AR.

The AK-47:

The AK-47 solved the difficult problem of firing thousands of rounds at approaching bad guys by allowing you to quickly change 30 round mags taped back to back. Unfortunately, getting one is difficult, as they only come fully-auto. The good news is that semi-automatic variants are available, allowing you to simulate an actual AK-47 by pulling the trigger really, really fast. Like the SKS, the AK functions best when filled with mud. Filling them is difficult though as the hi-cap magazine makes lying in a mud puddle while shooting very difficult. Another drawback of the AK is that it's not black. Fortunately, however, there's a black market for black. The AK also suffers from the troubling problem that its round is not .223 or .308, as Russian poodles are apparently no larger than American poodles.

I could go on and on, but I suggest you go to the URL and take it all in. It goes after handguns and caliber as well!

So now back to reality—It's up to us to sort this all out. The rifle is a Marauder's primary tool. An extension of his arm. A babe to sleep with at night. His guest at the dinner table. The #1 concern. So we need to get this one right.

As with handguns, in order to get the proper rifle we need to get our priorities straight. Those priorities are, in order:

1. Primary Use
2. Reliability
3. Durability
4. Accuracy
5. Weight (size, bulkiness, etc.)
6. Availability of Ammo

So let's examine this weapon's *primary use*. As you will read in Marauding 101, a lot of our work will be done at distances of about 50-150 yards. Outside the range of handguns, yet not so far out that we've become Snipers. We will be shooting from cover at defended targets over these distances. Mostly at night. This is our what our rifle will be helping us with. Fortunately there are plenty of weapons out there that can perform to this mission.

The next thing we need to examine is our rifle's *reliability*. A subset of this examination is ease of cleaning, maintenance and repair. We are going to be using and relying on this weapon for a long, long time. When we lock and load *it had better fire*. No jamming allowed. Dirt, dust, water, and if you've ever gone deer hunting in the northeast, ice, can ruin your whole day. Maybe even your weapon. By way of example, some guns, like the AK-47, shoot dirty. Really dirty. The AR-15, however, is a little more finicky. It prefers a cleaner environment. Kinda' like the classic muscle car debate—The 67' Shelby GT/AK you can drive for fifty miles over a pot-holed dirt road at 60mph and it will accelerate to 120 when you come off it and get on the highway. The Porsche 911 Turbo/AR, on the other hand, *will stop and put you through the windshield* if it even *feels* gravel under its tires, but will pop to 150 when it smells four-lane asphalt. Which do you prefer? Did I just confuse you all? (I don't read mail from Porsche owners).

My definition of *durability* is "Reliability" as described above, multiplied by years and years and thousands of rounds fired. Let's look at two classic rifles by way of example (whether you like their characteristics or not). The Winchester 94 (.30-30) and the AK-47. I think there have been something like 50 million AK's manufactured, and most of them are still in use today. Terrorists love them, of course. For good reason, as they eat mud, dirt, dust and sand. Comparably, I still shoot my first Winchester .30-30, given to me by my dad forty-four years ago. *44 years!* I can certainly attest to its durability-

These are the types of considerations we need to take into account here, as you won't be able to go out and buy "new" rifles or parts after the fall. These weapons need to work for the rest of your life!

When it comes to *accuracy* I think there's probably broad agreement among the Faithful. Again, let's use some well-known classics as a guide. At 300 yards:

1- You can shoot out somebody's eyeball with the AR-15
2- You'll *probably* hit him somewhere with the AK, and
3- You'll kick up a ton of dust around him with a .30-30.

Inside 200 yards:

4- A good shooter can knock out his eyeball with the AK

At 150 yards:

5- You can shoot out both eyeballs with a Winchester .30-30

Roughly and generally speaking, of course. Assuming you really know how to shoot. For our purposes though, I consider all of these weapons to be accurate.

Regarding *weight*, bulk, length, etc. this is a mess as well. The Marines carry the M4/AR-15 because when it's fully loaded and accessorized, it's pretty goddamned light for all the crap they're forced to hang off of it. The military moved to this weapon so that any infantryman could carry as much .223 ammo as humanly possible and still hump 20 miles. Try it sometime. It's not fun. That's why only the Infantry does it. Fully beautified it's probably around 10 pounds.

Hopefully we won't be humping 20 miles a day on a regular basis, but we will be on the move a lot. Mostly on foot (unless you've got *horse* power). We can probably handle 10 pounds if we need to. The AK-47 is a heavier weapon, around 10 pounds fully-loaded, but it doesn't come with all of the AR-15's trinkets. So 10 pounds is all you get. My .30-30 is about 7.5 pounds fully-loaded (with much less capacity, of course). But that little 2.5 pounds makes a huge difference on the trail, though-

Can you tell where I'm headed with all this?

There are obviously lots of rifles to choose from. And again, I don't mean for this book to be a technical treatise on weapons. I'm not that smart. I have done this before, however, and I've had the opportunity to real-world test some of the weapons I've been discussing. I would suggest, again, that if you have trouble sleeping at night go online and do a review of all kinds of rifles out there suitable for when the world goes to Hell. You might get more confused, actually.

So I will un-confuse you. Go get an AK-47 and a Winchester .30-30. I love the AR-15, and as I said earlier, I have a few of them, but they really are like exotic cars; with enough maintenance and support you get the optimum ride. In a post-apocalyptic scenario, however, that support or parts supply will not be available. So get the next best performer, the AK, a bit more rugged, durable, time and battle-tested. *Over 50 million produced*. Lots of ammo readily available, pre-and post-Fall of Civilization.

Okay, so now I've let on that my favorite handgun is a Russian Makarov and now I'm recommending the Kalashnikov. I also happen to be a fan of Russian women. My wife (number two) is Russian. Am I a Russian spy? Nope. The Russians just make great, simple, hardcore stuff. And I've had the misfortune of actually having had to use them in some very uncomfortable shitholes, so I know how they perform under duress.

My day gun would be the .30-30. Stick it in the saddle scabbard if you're riding. Very few moving parts. Tough as rocks. Will punch a hole through Level IV body armor. Is there any more readily available ammo? Probably not. I know I know it was my first gun and I'm biased; that doesn't mean I'm wrong. Was it Freud who first said that even hypochondriacs get sick? It's a damn great gun. It won the west, and after the Fall that's what this country might look like-

SHOTGUNS

When I hear the word "shotgun" I immediately think of Steve McQueen in "The Magnificent Seven" *riding it* up in the right front top seat of that horse-drawn hearse carriage, weapon in hand, sitting next to Yul Brynner as they head up the hostile main street of town to drop off a dead Indian up on Boot Hill . . . Sometimes I see my three kids in younger days running frantically to grab the front passenger seat in my car . . . Occasionally I'll think trap and skeet with my son . . . or ducks with my dad, a long, long time ago-

Rarely do I think about shotguns in an "offensive" sense. If you're not shooting birds or clays, or guarding a Wells Fargo stage, then you're generally thinking about a shotgun for *defensive* purposes. Generally home defense. And in some of those cases it works pretty well. Again, as you will read in Marauding 101, we will be operating in the great outdoors, mostly at night, so the shotgun holds minimal value for us. But we'll use it if we need to scare off a group of rag-tag raiders (though my inclination is to shoot them, usually), confront a pistol-wielding group outnumbering us, or if we're holding a specific target group at bay while we communicate our demands. In any of those situations, the psychological factor is paramount, and more specifically, the *intimidation factor.* And nothing is more intimidating than staring down a big sawed-off side by side with barrels the size of railroad tunnels and dual outside hammers like dragonheads pulled back and ready to breathe fire. Just thinking about it and I can feel the heat.

Why sawed-off?

So you actually don't have to aim it. This is actually a very good option for those of you that eventually find out that you really suck with a handgun . . .

Inside of thirty feet a 12-gauge sawed-off shotgun will hit just about everybody in that small group you might be pointing it at. I said *pointing*, not *aiming*, and that's the difference. One barrel should be enough, as the scatter can be a few feet wide. Both barrels, well, geez—if you need more than both barrels at that point then you probably shouldn't have been there in the first place.

However, given that this is the primary use for *our* shotgun, it probably won't get fired much at all. If we have to unload on a group that we're holding at bay with a sawed-off double barrel, something's gone horribly wrong. So I'm not going to go into a lot of detail comparing shotguns. Go online and take a look around, and if you like guns, they surely do make some pretty shotguns. But all we really need is a rugged old side by side. External hammers, to me, look a lot more intimidating, especially when the barrel is sawed-off. Winchester, Remington and Browning in the U.S., Baikal (Russia) and CZ-USA make some rugged guns as well. Get a 12 gauge. For those of you not familiar, those are some big-ass pellets in that shell. It'll shred your crowd to pieces at very close range. I recommend getting a used one, as cheap as possible, but make sure to see if it can handle steel shot (as opposed to lead), as we don't know what we'll be finding in the next life, and some older models have barrels that weren't hardened enough to handle steel.

A word about sawing off—as you might expect, I own an old Winchester, pretty well cut down. That's another 10 years in the federal pen for me, as it has a barrel less than 18 inches and an overall gun length of less than 26 inches. These are the current minimums for a shotgun. Anything else is a big felony (keep checking the law though as I'm not making any legal representations, again, here). You can cut any shotgun down legally, as long as when you're done it exceeds these dimensions (or whatever state and Federal regs demand). I own a fully legal CZ Coachgun as well. I own it because I think it's just a really beautiful weapon, and doesn't really need to be cut. Short of that, go online and you'll find some really good You-Tube videos detailing the saw-off process. It's pretty simple, hacksaw and filing, that's it. But if you usually try to avoid overnight visits to the federal pen, then save the sawing-off until right after the Fall.

BODY ARMOR

When it comes down to not getting killed or even severely wounded in a firefight, the only sure-fire action you can take is to actually *avoid one*. Which I recommend highly. They're not very much fun, really, and once you're in one, there ain't no getting out until it's over. You can't just say "Oops changed my mind!" or "Oh shit there's too many of em!'" and start running away. You just gotta tough it out. People actually die in these things.

So one of our universal maxims will be to stay as far away from our target as we can and still accomplish our objective. Among other universals, I'm a big believer in Murphy's Law, "Anything that can go wrong will go wrong," and some of it's ridiculous variations, like when you say "don't worry honey, I'll buy the Lotto tickets" then you forget and of course the numbers she wrote down for you were the winners, that kind of thing (I prefer the firefight!). Anyway, the farther away, the better. *Anything can and will go wrong when it's straight-up.* Your gun might *God Forbid* jam, or you get hit from behind, etc. etc. Unlike the Military, we cannot afford to take casualties. There aren't any more of us to fill in if we go down. We're not getting reinforcements. We won't be re-supplied. We're not going to keep fighting or keep coming back until we score. So if you encounter someone that needs to be taken out, and you can nail him at 500 yards with an AR-15, then do it. If you're lucky enough to have an ex-sniper in your crew who routinely scores at half a mile out, even better. If you have Tomahawk cruise missiles you can launch from a hundred miles away, well, you get the picture. No reason to ride up, call him out from fifty feet and say "Draw!" That's Hollywood-

So where am I going with this?

Get prepared for the worst, which includes getting caught by surprise, or biting off a little more than you can chew. You might have to take a few hits to get through it. That means protection. And I don't mean Trojans (unless you can resurrect a Legion of them). For this, you're gonna need Body Armor.

Formerly known as the flak jacket, then the bullet-proof vest, it has morphed into "bullet-resistant" (as nothing is 'proof' anymore except hard liquor) and now into "armor." I really don't know why. Maybe to make it sound tougher. Sounds more scary to me, though, because if those mentally-challenged Jihadists actually think I'm wearing Armor, they might use more armor-piercing rounds, which nothing you wear will save you from. But body armor is the name now so get used to it.

There's all different shapes and sizes of course, but the most important thing you need to know about armor is that it comes with five different levels of protection, as determined by the Deity blessed with determining a vest's viability, the National Institute of Justice, or "NIJ" for short. It is the US Department of Justice's research, development and evaluation agency. Somehow they got control of rating body armor, and actually rating it for the military (although the Military does its own testing as well). An important note is that it is always run by a political appointee of the President, so take that with a grain of salt. We've seen what Eric Holder has done for the Department of Justice. Your company's "rating" may be affected by your politics-

Anyway, these ratings are called "Levels of Protection" and they are, from weakest to strongest:

Level I (doesn't apply anymore)

Level IIa
Level II
Level IIIa
Level III
Level IV

Why in the 21st century we still use inefficient Roman Numerals is beyond me. Maybe it makes NIJ feel smarter. And usually, IIa would follow II, IIIa would follow III, etc. not the other way around. Maybe a clue as to why our DOJ is so screwed up-

You can read a whole lot of technical crap about standards, but in a nutshell:

- Level IIa will stop most 9mm and a .40 caliber S&W
- Level II will stop all 9mm, .40 and .357magnums
- Level IIIa will stop all of the above plus the .357 SIG with full metal jacket (FMJ) and the .44 magnum (with hollow points)
- Level III will stop all handguns you'll probably ever run into, all levels of buckshot, a 12-gauge slug. With ceramic plates also the AK-47.
- Level IV will stop everything above plus a .30 caliber. Once, maybe twice. You need to insert ceramic plates for this too, however.

The other important thing to understand about body armor is that it is really, really heavy. Level IV fully optioned can be 35 pounds. You wanna haul that around on your ass all day? I hope this gives you new appreciation for our boys in Afghanistan-

So here's the quandary: progressively higher levels of protection get progressively heavier, up to about 38 pounds. So we need to determine the most realistic threats we might face, the actions we will be taking, and weigh those against the impracticability of wearing that goddamned thing around all day.

As Marauders, roaming around mostly at night, I would opt for Level III when actually on a mission. It's going to be heavy enough as it is, but Shit Happens and we might run into a guy who can actually shoot the AR and hit stuff at 300 yards. At night. Once he dares fire at us, though, he's revealed himself and we'll take him out, but we don't want him to get lucky.

I would prefer not to wander around too much during the day, but if so I might opt for Level II. This is what most cops use. I know that I am smarter than to expose myself 300 yards out in broad daylight and get taken down by the AR or AK. I'll take my chances against handguns and you can bet your ass I won't get inside a shotgun's window. At some point we need to kick back, though, just a little—Level II !

NIGHT VISION

I know you all think this is magic, but it's really a just parlor trick. Night vision goggles, whether binocular or monocular, are really just glorified magnifying glasses. The difference being they magnify ambient (existing, natural) light.

Example—you're backpacking in the Needles, in southern Colorado, around 9000 feet. It's a beautifully starry night, with about a quarter of a moon hanging out up there. You can see all that bright beauty in the sky. This is ambient light. You can hardly see it, however, when it reflects off the trees, rocks, dirt, etc., at ground level though—That's where the goggles do their thing. They magnify that reflected ambient light a gazillion times so that you can easily see (relatively speaking) what that light is reflecting from (a tree, a deer, or SURPRISE! a Green Beret standing there ready to gut you).

Beware, however, that as they magnify light a gazillion times, it is inadvisable then to stare into a non-ambient light source while wearing night vision goggles. You might get blinded. *No, really.*

That said, I'm not a big fan of Night Vision. It must be calibrated for distance, so it's a pain in the ass if you're trying to move around in the brush with em' on, looking out for danger, and constantly adjusting. You'll probably make a ton of noise, give yourself away then get shot dead as a result. The field of vision can be pretty narrow as well, and determining people from tree stumps takes some experience. Oh and did I mention batteries? I prefer to rely on my natural, God-given night vision, combined with my natural hearing. I've gotten pretty good at using them. You can too.

As a laser targeting system, however, it's pretty damn simple and easy to use. Once you've identified your target, you just line up that little' ol' infrared dot on it and those goggles make that little dot look like a sunrise! Just like with your digital camera, *point and shoot!* Works every time!

FLIR

Forward-Looking-Infrared. That's what it means. Way better than ordinary Night Vision goggles, however. These devices (usually something resembling those old, clunky Sony Handycams from back in the 80's) are magnifying glasses as well. Only with these you get heat magnification, hence the term "Heat Vision."

Same theory as that of Night Vision, a magnification of ambient heat. The difference with this technology, of course, is that not all of the objects in your field of view may be giving off heat. Which makes a warm body on a cold night stand out like a full moon against the dark sky. Contrast that with Night Vision, where just about everything is reflecting some ambient light, screwing up your field of view, and you can tell why FLIR can be a very useful tool. Straight up, if you're out and about in a relatively open area on a cool night you're gonna get shot, no doubt about it, if anybody hunting you has them.

The good news for you is that you probably won't run into anybody who does. As with Night Vision, I'm not a huge fan. Don't misread what I'm writing, though. These things really work! *Their problems outweigh their usefulness,* however. The reliable FLIR devices are REALLY EXPENSIVE, you need *batteries* and maintenance is a *huge* problem. You (or your enemies) won't get much use out of them before they fail. They don't work well in wet, muddy or even icy conditions. The military does not standard-issue them, so you can see where this is going. Special Ops guys have them, but remember, they have very defined missions, very specific planning, they can call a NO-GO at any time, start again, and get issued new units at the first sign of trouble. You won't have that luxury. Neither will those you come up against.

But if you suspect your opponent has FLIR, you beat them by staying in cover (as you always should), wearing your armor, and moving in teams (always) so if a shot is fired your crew can locate the shooter and take him out immediately. Again, if it's a bunch of ex-Navy SEALs, well, then you're shit out of luck anyway.

Use those thousands of dollars on rifles and ammo instead.

TEAR GAS

Well again yes we can and well no we can't—Some states allow it, some don't. I have a bunch of it, of course, but in California I'm allowed to own it. The fines are small (a grand) for misusing it, which means threatening somebody with it, and although they can throw you in the Federal Penalty Box for actually using it, I've never heard of it happening. So as I'm not gonna need it until after the Fall, I keep acquiring it. Check your state and local jackboots if you're scared of getting caught with it.

Now, really, do I have to write about what the Hell to do with this? Ok, for the uninitiated, this will burn and temporarily blind the shit out of your eyes and sear your lungs and throat until you wish you were dead. If you try to stay in a cloud and tough it out then you will be dead, either by suffocation from the lack of oxygen or from the fact that it has the effect of shoving a fully-erect bull's cock into your esophagus. So run away. *Fast.* And that is what your targets will do. Get a canister into their safe place and they're gone. Flush 'em out like you're bird-hunting. Then shoot them. Really. That's what you use it for. Hopefully you'll be able to think up *on your own* the hundreds of scenarios in which its possible use can occur. It is a precious commodity, however, and when it's gone, it's gone. Highly unlikely you'll find it anywhere after the Fall. That's why we complement tear gas with:

AMMONIA, BLEACH and OVEN CLEANER

This stuff, of course, is great for cleaning up wounds and killing germs (and with your rationing of water supplies after the Fall, sanitation is a HUGE issue). But they're also basic and simple tools in the Anarchist's Cookbook (google) for making poison gas and low-powered (but deadly) explosive devices. So these are two-for-one'ers.

Most housewives and Mexican cleaning crews are smart enough to know not to mix ammonia and bleach. College kids, not so much—Doing so creates Chlorine Gas. Really. The same shit they used in both World Wars. Inhaling only a small amount of it will tear into your nasal passages, trachea and lungs, cause unbearable amounts of pain and blood, and screw up your breathing for life. And it gets worse, depending upon your mix. Too much bleach and there's a good possibility it will explode in your face, so do I really have to tell you why this is bad? Add significantly more ammonia than bleach and you end up with rocket fuel, but with a little bit of a delayed explosion. So if you're going to use these chemical weapons, make sure you add the right amounts for your purposes. Toward the end of this book I outline scenarios in which I employ them.

Oven cleaner is one of the great little misunderstood products of our time. It is The Little Engine That Could. Not only has it stepped-up and saved millions of housewives from Carpal Tunnel and arthritis, but it also had grand ambitions of being a real big-boy explosive. Which it is. *If only we would use him, he would prove it!* Well here we do. Mix a little shredded aluminum foil with Oven Cleaner, wait 15 seconds and BOOM! The Little Explosive That Could. Choose your usage wisely.

BACKPACKING EQUIPMENT

Well, again, this is pretty obvious. Marauders are on the move, and the best way to do it is with superlightweight gear. If you have horses, you can get more stuff or heavier stuff or be redundant. Whatever works for you. As I mentioned in Chapter 2, Go to REI or North Face and they will be happy to outfit you. My only suggestions would be that everybody have their own 2-man tent, their own water filter (preferably 2) and their own stove.

WATER FILTERS

Regarding filters, my preference here goes to durability. Like your handguns and rifles, you might be relying on it for a long, long time. Don't cheap-out on this item. Do some research based on your budget, but start with Katadyn. I have the top of the line model, surgically pure water, works for twenty years. There are other good ones as well, I'm just partial, having used it a lot.

PORTABLE SOLAR CHARGERS

A word about solar chargers—What the hell are you going to use them for? Think about it—Night Vision or Heat Vision? Laser? Then you'll need to find something that will have the ability to charge all of these devices centrally, preferably from one unit. Some of the more dependable and powerful ones can be expensive (and heavy). So figure out how you think you will be operating in the next life, and acquire the unit(s) you think apply. As with everything else, you'll never get a consensus. I've got a big strong crew, and we ride, so I bring a bigger unit. I recommend one per party. Go online and figure it all out.

TRIAGE KIT, MATCHES, LIGHTERS, ROAD FLARES

Ok no explanation needed, except for two things:

1. You won't be stopping cars roadside with the flares. They're for igniting explosives, setting a structure on fire, etc.
2. Build the Triage kit to the highest level of expertise in your crew. Nothing more, nothing less. You got a guy who can amputate? Make sure you have the right equipment, pain killers and meds. Best you can do is a splint? Well, sorry-

KILKENNY

GASOLINE, EMPTY WINE AND BEER BOTTLES

Well obviously these are not for drinking and driving! This is for making Molotov Cocktails (as opposed to 5 O'clock cocktails).

If you've never made or used one, at the very least you've probably heard of them. Maybe you don't know what they really are, so once again for the uninitiated-

A Cocktail or Molotov is basically a weapon of intimidation with very little destructive value on it's own. It is primarily used to disperse a reasonable area of flame onto an object, vehicle, roof, your neighbor's poodle, etc. It does very little damage itself but, of course, can ignite something that will cause significant damage. Gasoline vapors burn out pretty quickly, although if you catch paper, some flammable curtains, or some really snappy dry wood, they might ignite. Obviously if it ignites another more powerful combustible material you're in trouble.

As I mentioned, I use them primarily as an intimidation/psychological warfare tool, because if you've never had one come crashing through your window, I guarantee that the first time it happens it will make you sweat-

Here's how they work: an easily breakable glass bottle is filled with gasoline. 3/4ths full. A teaspoon of motor oil is added if you want the flames to stick on something a little longer, but it's not necessary. A rag soaked in kerosene, lighter fluid, etc. is shoved into the bottle neck, making contact with the gasoline. Put some kind of stopper to hold it in place. The rag is lit, the bottle tossed, and when the bottle smashes, it is the small gasoline droplets that disperse into the air mixed with the gasoline vapor that ignites, creating an immediate fireball, followed by an intense fire consuming the rest of the gasoline. That's it. It's that simple. Relatively safe. Terrorists and idiot college kids rarely if ever set themselves on fire using them.

You really won't need anything more than this, but some people can get pretty creative. The only modification or upgrade that I might suggest, is that if you add a bit more motor oil and some dishwashing liquid, you'll get a stickier substance that produces thick, black smoke. Something to think about if you have a different objective or if you want to spare your tear gas or bleach-

DOGS

These are a personal preference, of course, but also a valuable tool. Most of these Doomsday Prepper fools rely on their dogs for protection, going out and getting German Shepherds, Dobermans, Rotts, etc. to protect them from bad guys. Well, good luck with that. You'll see why in a later chapter.

As in all of our most important equipment choices, breed is also personal choice. Importantly, though, we also need to determine the dog's primary mission. For me, and in my experience, I don't need a dog to protect me; I need a dog to be my alarm system. If something's up, I want a smart enough dog to pick it up, identify it and figure it out, then come and communicate that information to me. I love Dobermans and have had quite a few, but they go barking off at stuff that they haven't quite figured out, which can be good, but I'd rather they let me know first. Rotts are the opposite. They might let someone in the house knowing then they will then tear his leg off. But I might not necessarily know that. And they don't understand bullets. Great dogs, but not what I need. My German Shepherd is a little of both; he'll do that quiet "Whoof," when something catches his attention, then moves quietly around to get a better look. This usually gets my ears up. He'll go at it, though, when he figures it out, but I'm usually ready by then.

So I would take the German Shepherd over the other dogs just discussed. I don't think too many of you would argue with me too much about that choice. Where you all might think I'm nuts is with my true, absolute first choice of dog in the world, the Border Collie. These beautiful little 45 pound dogs will not strike fear even in the heart of a small child, but they are far and away *the smartest dogs on the planet by a wide margin*. Some of them have vocabularies of a thousand words! That's not a dog, that's a crewmember! In addition they are also the quickest, most athletic and durable dogs out there. 20 miles a day, every day, easy-

My border collies will sense something, then quietly come get me. Usually it's a coyote or a stranger on the property. One of them usually stays in position or follows until I tell them to stand down. Amazing! Real Security Guards. They give me control of the information, the situation, then I make the decisions, not them.

I also use the shepherd and Border Collies as the perfect recon and flush mechanisms. I give the command to the BC's to sniff around, and then they all go look for concealed shooters. They also love to chase any ball thrown, so, unfortunately, if I think an area I need to pass through is booby-trapped, I start throwing the tennis ball. Had an accident once, but so far haven't lost one. This is really about *human* survival though, so better them than me. *Reluctantly-*

HORSES

As I wrote in Chapter 2, a horse will probably become the primary means of transportation again after the Fall, and is the perfect all-weather, all-terrain vehicle. Especially at night. Again, I'm not advocating going out and buying them now, hell no. If you have some already, great. If you don't, learn to ride. After the Fall you'll see how easy it will be to acquire them. They will make your marauding life much more interesting, pleasurable, comfortable and efficient.

OK WHERE DO WE STORE ALL THIS CRAP

This is a difficult question, with lots of answers based upon what your ultimate marauding profile will be. The best situation to be in is if you become the type that has a base of operations, working out from there. However, that puts you at risk of becoming a target, just like everyone else. Multiple bases of operation are best, never hanging around an area for more than a month or so on any one rotation.

Needless to say you should take all of the essentials with you when you leave on a mission, and leave only the exotics/spares back at base. But somewhere in your territory you need to bury a couple of big gun safes, with mechanical locking bolt actions. These will be big enough to hold the bulk of your essentials, and you can scatter the non-essentials about. They are really heavy, so just below ground level is fine, nobody's going to steal them. Or blow the mechanism off.

Two things you will need to protect against: Moisture outside and moisture inside. Outside is easy, of course, because just about all of the quality units come fire-resistant, and fire-resistance brings with it a bit of water resistance as well. In addition I would use about 20 cans of that rubber spray can pipe repair stuff they advertise on TV, it works really well. Pretty much encases it in waterproofing rubber. The bigger problem is inside the safe. You need to load it up with silica gel. You ever see those little salt-packet looking things in some medicine bottles? Those are silica packs, meant to absorb moisture. Load up. As long as your guns are oiled, greased and siliconed, you're all set.

OK LAST BUT MOST IMPORTANT !!

BALLS

Big ones. Not tennis balls for the dogs, either. A man's real stones, Cojones! You're absolutely going to need them. If yours are not big enough just yet, go work them out. Just like working your brain, or exercising your muscles, or stuffing your belly eating a high-carb, high-fat diet, you *can* make them bigger. Really. Go back to Chapter two. Please.

CHAPTER 5

Marauding 101

Well, everybody, this is where we get to the drive behind this book: Learning how to accomplish the Objective-

Identifying the things you want and/or need, then developing and executing a plan to go out and get them.

Drawing Some Inspiration

I will spare you the unnecessary platitudes from Sun-Tzu or Von Clausewitz that others may be tempted to write about at this point. That said, before we go at it there are some words of advice that have survived for a long time because, well, they're actually true. I know for a fact that I am not smarter than any of these guys quoted below (except Marcinko), so I've applied these maxims to my own life and exploits. *Successfully.* I recommend you do so as well. If you don't know these guys, Google them. I suggest you memorize these words, and take heed; Doom will rain down upon you if you don't-

> "Do not sleep under a roof. Carry no money or food. Go alone to places frightening to the

> common brand of men. Become a criminal of purpose. Be put in jail and extricate yourself by your own wisdom."
> -Miyamoto Musashi, <u>The Book of Five Rings</u> 1645

This is the "Marauder's Creed" Dammit!

I'm glad that I read this book back when I was 17. Get out there and test yourself. Feel some fear. Deal with it. Start now. Get used to failure. Learn to adapt. Learn how to win. Don't wait until it all goes to Hell someday-

> "Two things are infinite: the Universe and Human stupidity. And I'm not sure about the Universe."
> -Albert Einstein, 1943

Einstein is, well, Einstein! Please avoid Human stupidity-

> "The more thou sweateth in training, the less thou bleedeth in combat."
> -Dick Marcinko, Founder of Seal Team Six

Dick Marcinko is no Einstein, but was perhaps one of the five most dangerous men on the planet in his prime. He's spot-on here: you need to train. The more the better. It doesn't matter if your enemy trains less. It will pay off.

> "Anything that can go wrong, will go wrong."
> -Captain Edward Murphy, USAF 1948

This is my favorite Law of The Universe, and I am a true believer. It's happened to me a hundred times. Adapt, Adapt, Adapt, as your plan goes awry, or you will die. It's as simple as that. Ask Dick Marcinko about Murphy as well-

This next maxim is a great follow-up:

> "When I don't have red, I use blue."
> -Pablo Picasso, 1953

Perhaps the greatest of all time takes what is there, changes his plan, adapts, improvises, executes, and then creates a Masterpiece! I love this guy! As I've said many times, *Shit Happens!* so we all need to become masters of improvisation in order to create masterpieces.

Okay last but maybe should also be first as well, this is *deadly important* to anyone after the Fall:

> "A man's got to know his limitations."
> -Detective Harry Callahan, aka Dirty Harry, 1973

The greatest sin you can commit is *overconfidence.* You discover that you totally suck with a handgun? Carry a sawed-off shotgun. You don't have any good body armor? Learn to shoot the AK from 300 yards. *At night.* There's a bunch of ex-Marines guarding your targeted ranch? Walk on by. Leave them be. Let the sleeping Devil Dogs lie. Move on to the easier targets. A man's got to know his limitations.

Rules For The Road

The Maxims I've outlined above become our intellectual and spiritual guide to success after the Fall of Society. I've summarized them into our Rules for The Road. Literally.:

1. Become a man of purpose
2. Challenge your fear
3. Avoid stupid mistakes
4. Learn. Train. Hard.
5. Shit Happens. *A Lot*
6. Adapt your plan when necessary
7. Use Blue
8. Know your limitations

Let's get it going-

As I've mentioned before, Marauding is not about roaming about and robbing anybody we see just because we have guns and they don't; and it's not about taking advantage of those idiot Doomsday Preppers (although I consider them to be low-hanging fruit). Staying alive, and living the best quality of life we can provide to ourselves and whomever else we deem worthy is what we should, and can, accomplish. This is what it's about. At the risk of being boring *Again!* I do NOT believe in rape or murder. That's not to say that some people don't need killing, or that I haven't killed anybody, as of course some do, and of course I have. Murder is different. That's killing an innocent for no good reason. Innocents do get killed, of course, but usually with good reason. For non-innocents we will need no reason—I know I'll get mail about this vs. my past. I can live with it.

Make no mistake, people are going to get killed, be killed, and get raped and murdered in the next life. If you don't believe that as Gospel, then quit reading now and use this book instead of firewood for your cozy fireplace. You're an idiot who can't be saved.

We will avoid killing innocents at all costs. Our objective is Lifestyle, Food and Accouterments (too big a word for you all?). Not dominance. Not Empire-building. Not Control. If that's what you're after then don't bother reading any further and go find some Nazi site on the web. There's plenty of that crap around—We're Pros, and we will be approaching this as such and in a business-like fashion.

Speaking of Approach

In order to become a pro at this game and to maximize the use of your time, effort and equipment in order to reap the richest rewards, keep in mind that this endeavor is a *business*. That's not to say that you may not have some personal scores to settle in the next life; that's okay. But for what we're trying to accomplish here, let's keep emotion out of it as much as possible (I struggle with this too but *I'm trying*). It can't completely go away, of course, as everything is personal if you're involved in it. We just need to keep it at bay.

That in mind, here's the ten-step outline of the science of Marauding:

1. Objective
2. Reconnaissance
3. Identifying Multiple Targets of Opportunity
4. Qualifying Each Opportunity
5. Target Selection
6. Goals for Each Target
7. Planning the Operation
8. Staging The Order of Operations
9. Implementation and Execution
- First *Move, Psychological Warfare*
- *Second Move, Intimidation*
- *Third Move, Attack Prep*
- *Fourth Move, Attack*
- *Fifth Move, Assessment*
10. Post-Operation Follow-up

Seems simple, right? Well some of it is, some of it isn't—Before we dive into each of these steps it's important to point out here that the two most dangerous times in this whole 10-step process are at the beginning and at the end—during Reconnaissance and Post-Op follow-up. Kind of like during takeoff and landing of any commercial flight. *Why, you say? Wouldn't it be more dangerous during Implementation?* Well, no. Implementation and Execution are the easy parts. As you will learn, a big part of our offensive will be psychological; and the parts that aren't will have been outlined, studied and understood by all of us so that we control information, dictate timing, control the action, etc. Reconnaissance is just that—We don't know what the hell we're dealing with just yet, so we better be really goddamned careful as we go find out. Again, a potential target might be guarded by Green Berets who've melted into the landscape ready to pop up out of the dirt like Whack-a-Moles and slit your throat. *I hate when that happens. Ruins your whole day.* Same thing on the back end, when we re-visit the site of the Operation. We don't know what's gone on since we went away. We're almost back at Recon again.

Let's use another real-world situation from my past as guide-

CHAPTER 6

The Road to Leon'

The following story has been posted on my website in the past, as it is a great example of the incorporation of all ten steps outlined in the previous chapter. This was an operation conducted solely by me, with some resources supplied by a local Agency contact. If you've forgotten what I did for a living, read "About Me" again. Once you finish it, we'll break it down-

In the late 70's and throughout the 80's Latin America was a mess, and one of the messiest countries in it was Nicaragua. The entire Contra operation was in full swing, and the region was starting to feel some of the side effects. Collateral damage you could call it. You supply enough weapons and money to enough guys willing to get killed with them, and, well, *Shit Happens!* Not always the kind you intend, either. The U.S. was accomplishing its objective of destabilization throughout the region, for sure, but rogue elements causing trouble among the locals is always a usual side effect of this type of activity.

I was working on some legitimate banking business in Bogota' when I got a call from one of my Agency contacts in Mexico City. Seems he'd been hearing a bit of chatter from Managua about a spree of kidnappings and rapes down there, with the government hanging it on the Contras, of course. Probably was true. Too much negative press was already burning ears in D.C., so somehow they had to get a lid on it. He inquired as to whether I was interested. I was. I would have done it for free, but the cash price was good. Whether I believe in a certain cause or not, kidnapping, and especially rape, makes my blood boil to the point of instant insanity. They're the ultimate acts cowardice, of control and dehumanization. It really, really, pisses me off. My contact in Mexico City may have known this about me at the time, maybe not. But I wasn't going to turn down a chance to check it out.

The next day I checked out of the Hotel Tequendama in Bogota', but left my stuff with a baggage boy I knew well. It had all my business clothes, shoes, Ray-Bans, etc. I gave him $20 bucks to take it to his house, and would pay him $30 bucks to pick it up again. We'd done this before. I didn't want to leave my bags checked-in at the hotel then come back and see the front desk guy wearing one of the ties my mom gave me last Christmas!

That evening I landed in Managua wearing ratty old Lee blue jeans I used for this type of stuff, a black T-shirt and beat-up old pair of Adidas tennis shoes. Crappy old Aviators too. Nice gold chain. I've got two full days growth going on my face now, and being dark with longish dark hair to begin with, pulling it straight back I slid right in with my beat up Eurofag overnight bag, Mexican Passport and mucho Dolores'. I took a cab over to El Hotel Pasarela (the Runway Hotel) near the airport, as the taxistas would always take a shortcut into town at night *where you could count on "Police Inspections," which usually cost foreigners jaunts to local ATM's to clear any "contraband."* That's actually funny. *Contra-banned.* Anyway, the driver ripped me off, of course, but I wasn't there to bring the wrath of Zeus down upon him. I'm trying to maintain a low profile, lay low, wait for my contact.

I check into El Pasarela, and it's more like a Mexican whorehouse (there's a difference from other ones, believe me) than a hotel. It's got some funky-toothed Nicaraguan tough guy in the "lobby," with that stupid rack of keys hanging on hooks behind an old wood bar subbing for the check-in counter, which of course he's not at. He's lying on a shitty brown couch off to the side of the entry watching Futbol' on the little black and white on a small coffee table. A couple of prostitutes sitting around on guys' laps on the other two shitty sofas in the lobby. Everybody's smokin' dope. I like that. It's easier to take out a guy that's stoned, rather than one on coke. I'll also take belligerent drunks before cokeheads. They're all smiling too.

I'll spare you the translation here, but it's like 'Hombre, you want a room with some ass? I say no, just a room. Mr. Futbol mumbles 'maricon Mexicano' and everybody laughs, me too. He just called me a faggot and my Spanish always sounds Mexican, he got that too. Everybody's in a good mood though, so he gets up takes $25 from me and gives me the key to room 237. And room 230.

Ok I get it now. I thought my contact in Mexico was sending a guy in the morning, but this is him! I walk up the creaky-ass wood stairs covered by a beer and bloodstained red runner, in full view of the crowd. They see me open the door to 237 and walk in.

I dump the fag bag and start looking. 10 minutes later and there it is, covered in piss and paper and shit in the toilet. A .38 Special, hermetically sealed in a plastic bag. *Another shitty job!* I get it out, clean off the bag, open the window wide to the balcony, maybe ten feet above the ground. Then I promptly exit 237 through the connecting door to 235, lock the connecting door behind me, walk through the hallway door out of view of the partying patrons down below, and slip quietly down the hall into room 230. Of course they came to 237 in the middle of the night, looking for my Dolares. But I was sound asleep, .38 in hand, in room 230.

In the morning I re-read the note that came with the gun. The bus to Leon at 0800. That means 8am. Ok another rip-off taxi ride to the bus station, onto the bus to Leon.

It smells like dogshit. Literally. There's a dog in the seat behind me, a pitbull, that just shit on the floor. Nobody cares. It's one of those old 60's kind of school buses, with drapery and baubles and crap hanging off the inside windows and postcard pictures of Jesus touching his exposed heart and the Blessed Virgin radiating sunbeams taped up all around. The outside of the bus is painted red and white. Everybody's luggage is tied onto a giant roof rack. Chicken coops included. What a fucking' job!! It's filled with Nicaraguan locals, mostly older men and old ladies, a few pretty young girls, and two blonde chicks. There's also two younger, darker, more savvy-looking guys wearing mirrored-aviators on it too. *Trouble.*

DOOMSDAY MARAUDERS

We're headed out maybe an hour or so, and the Savvy guys have been chatting with all the pretty little girls on the bus. The Blondes too. From the chitchat I hear that the Blondes are Peace Corps workers taking a few days break and headed back to Honduras. *Funny those guys spoke English to them.* Or maybe not—The local girls are just that, headed home to either the coffee or cotton fields up outside of Leon. Poor, hard-working, but cute. And young-

Usually buses like these pull over by little roadside shacks selling Coca-Cola, water and Twinkies where you could get out and use the glorified outhouse if you needed to. Not this bus. In broad daylight, middle of the day, we round a corner staring off at a beautiful view of the volcano-mountains, and pull over on a widened part of the road near a heavily treed slope. It's that mesquite-type shit that's hard to push through. *So this is it.*

"Everybody out!" the bus driver barks. Go do what you need to do, he says. He's about 65, bald crown surrounded by silver, big fat moustache. Size 38 waist on a guy 5'6. Not dressed too shabbily though—Reluctantly, I wrap my passport and the .38 in a sock and shove it into and under the pitbull shit, and smear some extra shit over it. I'm winging this, but I'm goddamn sure somebody's coming. Maybe for the money, maybe for the girls, but I'm pretty sure not for me-

As soon as the guys are done pissing along the road and the old ladies are done squatting in the treeline, out they come. Two guys, dressed pretty much like me, but with bandanas covering their faces. They're holding S&W 9mm's; one has an AK-47. *Contras! Regular road thugs don't have this type of firepower.*

I'd been exposed to other Contras before, of course. But that was in a military capacity, and another story. These guys have gone off the reservation. They start interrogating us, very cool and calm, and start taking everybody's shit. Wallets, chains, necklaces, rings. They start chatting with the Savvy guys, *in English!* Why? Ostensibly nobody around there understands them. Except me. I can't hear all of it, though, but enough. These guys are pretty sharp for a bunch of dumbasses. *They've culled the herd.* The Blondes are off-limits. Peace Corps. That will bring Marines quicker than shit as these are mostly the kids of US government employees. The other cute little Nicaraguan girls are good to go, except one. I don't know why, and I never found out. They tell the bus driver to go get everybody's shit from off the bus, he does, and they take it all. There wasn't much, of course. This is just for show. They're really here for the girls. Nobody will come looking for them, and being *that* young, they're worth *a lot!*

They split the pack and some of the men protest, only to get a pistol-whip of 9mm metal. I give those guys credit, though. I'll always remember that. They spoke out. Against the odds. *Some of us still have balls, I think*—I helped one of the guys up, and as I'm of course much taller than all of them, at 5'11, I'm noticed again. One of the little prick Contras looks at me and says "Eh HEH gringo, what're you doing way the fuck out here." *In English.* I ignore him, like I don't understand. He approaches, I'm getting tight . . . He gets right in my face, and my instinct is to take him out right there, but I'm sure one of the others will get me. *Cool, boy, Cooooool . . .* "Que su problema chingach!!" I bark in Spanish as I shove him back and then get the pistol whipping. Took a good crack up under my left eyebrow, knocked me down, almost knocked me out. That's gonna leave a mark. And it's bleeding like shit. "Eh HEH! Chingach? Un Maricon Mexicano!!" he barks out. 'Chingach' means fuck-off in Mexican. He's imitating me. And he called me a faggot (What the hell is this? *Twice now!* Do I really look like a faggot?). "Camine!" He yells. Let's go. With that bandana I still can't see his face, but I won't forget him. And if I get the chance, *I will kill that motherfucker.* We all get on the bus, and as we drive off, an old purple Jeep Wagoneer pulls up to the gang left behind, but we're around the corner and gone, before they leave . . . Now the men are grumbling, old ladies swearing. They know the cops won't do anything. The Blondes are crying loudly and having a nervous breakdown. *For Christ's sake shut the fuck up! My head is killing me!*

Jumping ahead a bit. We finally get to Leon, I get a big band aid for my face, get some dinner in a decent bar (with strippers), catch all kinds of shit from the locals about how bad I must've got my ass kicked, stay in another shit hotel near the bus station (I think it was named ShitAss) and hop a bus back to Managua the next morning. *No unanticipated stops.* When I get back to the Runway Hotel in Managua out by the airport I quietly inquire about getting a Kodak instamatic with my contact, the 'manager.' He obliges within a few hours. I drop it in my fag bag and head out.

Baldy the bus driver isn't too hard to find. When I got off at the terminal in Managua I told some of the workers there I had some money for him. I needed his address. It only cost me $20 — I knew it was real because the guy sees my fucked-up face and realizes it could be him, and now I know where he works. I hop *ANOTHER* asshole cab and get out about a quarter mile from Baldy's house. Little kids in uniforms are piling down this street now, all bouncy-bouncing home from school. Kids are the same everywhere, in every town, in every country. It's a great thing to see—I saunter by Baldy's address in this better-than-average low income neighborhood. Pretty clean, no wild-ass dogs running around. Actual sidewalks. The door to his house is right next to an auto repair garage (it seemed to me that this is the only business in Latin America). A cute little black-haired Nicaraguan girl, about 10, knocks on Baldy's door and SNAP SNAP SNAP I've got her picture right as Baldy opens it and she yells Popi! and they close the door. *Christ that was easy.* It's an instamatic, so the photos are developing as I'm walking quickly away, camera and photos back in the fag bag.

At the bus station I had also found out that Baldy was driving back to Leon in the morning, so I better get a good night's sleep. *It's gonna be a long day-*

I'm up at 0600, shower, shave, cut my own hair off. Part it down the side. Pull a new purple Izod shirt out of the fag bag with a pair of khaki shorts and the old addidas'. They have a couple of my blood drops on them, so I wash 'em off, but they look pretty damned good! A new pair of sunglasses, black frame, black lenses. Man, I am the ultimate *Maricon!* Toss the fag bag over my shoulder, stuff the .38 into my left front pocket, and head over to Baldy's bus.

Baldy looks a little jumpy today. Probably because some big greasy Mexican-looking dude was looking for his address yesterday, offering cash, yet nobody owes him any money, so he's wondering—I'm slouching a little, and nobody recognizes me. *I hope!* I'm speaking now in my happy voice, in English, actually hoping they think I'm queer. I sure *feel* queer, but I know that's the adrenaline rush. Two days ago it was *recon*—this is now the *takeout*—so I'm nervous, edgy, but really, really ready. "Hello Sir!" I sing-song out to Baldy as I board the bus, dead last. He sneers at me, and I know he's thinking, *Maricon!* Good. Step one, on the bus—I take in the surroundings instantly. Pretty much the same makeup as the other day, only difference being an American couple on the bus too, they don't speak Spanish, but no Blondes. The two Savvy guys are there as well. I take the seat right behind one of them and happily sing "Hi Sir!" as I drop into the seat. He's sneering at me too. I start humming to myself, just loud enough so that people around me catch a little bit of it. Good. Step two, great positioning, they think I'm a total faggot.

The Savvy guys are at it again, doing their thing. I can hear the American couple talk about how long it's been since they've talked with anybody back home. *Oh, ok you stupid fucks. Just send a goddamn telegraph that nobody's looking for you or knows where the hell you are! For Christ's sake doesn't anybody read the news? It's fucking civil war around here and they think it's cool. What the fuck is wrong with these idiots?* Well, they're *Canadian*, it turns out, as I can tell by their accents. And they are goddamned lucky they got on *my* bus that day—The Savvy guys finish their recon and sit back in their seats a few minutes before we reach the Curve.

Just like the other day, Baldy turns the big curve and pulls the bus off the road onto the dirt parking sway. He's stands up and yells the same shit at us to get off the bus. Mr. Savvy in front of me stands up as I PULL THE .38 FROM MY POCKET POP! BAM! RIGHT THROUGH THE BACK OF HIS HEAD THERE'S SCREAMING SAVVY #2 TURNS IN POP!CRACK! TIME TO CATCH IT IN THE THROAT BLOWING OUT THE WINDOW BEHIND HIM SCREAMING EVERYBODY SCREAMING I LEVEL AIM ON BALDY-

All of the passengers are on the floor, screaming, crying, some in shock, others like 'hey, what the fuck, it's Nicaragua.' The Canadian idiots are looking at me like I'm *El Diablo*, eyes as wide as sewer pipes. I'm still aiming at Baldy, who's still standing. "Señor?," I'm speaking to Baldy in Spanish, quietly, calmly, no longer in my happy voice. This is my angry voice. The bus is dead silent. He looks a little pissed-off. "If you have a gun please show me. He does. A .38, like mine. Only older, maybe hasn't been fired in a while—In Spanish I tell everyone what is about to happen. They're starting to panic. "Calme' SE," calm DOWN, It will be ok. "Let's get off the bus and go huddle in the treeline." I walk up to Baldy and toss the Kodak photo of his daughter at him. "La tenemos." We have her, I tell him. If I don't come back, she dies. He pees the front of his pants, starts crying . . . Dumb fuck. I know now he won't say anything—Both of the Savvy boys had 9mm's, and although I'd prefer shooting with them, I'll stick to the revolver as I know where it came from. For all I know the Savvy's mags might jam, or they haven't cleaned them, whatever. They're assholes, for Christ's sake!

"And you're a murderer" the Canadian woman barks at me, crying. Of course she has no idea what's going on, but it still pissed me off. I was tempted then to shoot her as well, but I settled for a good backhanded bitch slap instead! "Shut the fuck up" I said. Her husband said nothing. *"They're coming."*

First one out of the treeline is the guy with the AK. It must be his personal weapon. He walks around holding it tight like it's his hard-on. Then I hear "Eh HEH! hola amigos," it's the little prick that pistol-whipped me in the face—Now *I'm getting a hard-on*—He comes waltzing over in that fake jovial tone, then goes dead silent—he's looking for the Savvys—"Donde 'stan Gordito?" he says to Baldy. Called him little fat boy! HA! How funny! That little prick is still about 20 yards from me, a little far for a head shot. And he stops. "No estan aqui hoy" they didn't come today, Baldy answers. The little prick is clearly nervous about this, scanning all of us, his rat-like little eyes jiggering wildly around. I know he can't hit me from there, but the AK can. I need to take that out first. Then I'll take my chances. I bet the little prick never shot anything out past 5 feet-

Well, as I've said before, *Shit Happens!* The AK notices the bus window, bloody and blown out! *Crap! I didn't think about that! God Dammit. He starts running toward the bus within 20 feet of me close enough I jump up* PUMP A ROUND ABOVE AND THRU HIS RIGHT EAR THEN TURN THE LITTLE PRICK IS FIRING MISSING I STICK ONE LEFT SHOULDER HE SPINS ANOTHER ONE INTO HIS SPINE BAM!CRACK! *and he-is-fucking-dead.*

Almost blew the whole damn thing with that window! *Got lucky*—OK we hurry now because the Jeep Wagoneer that dropped the bandana guys off should be coming back soon. "Everybody on the bus" I yell, and tell Baldy to get going—*and to tell the assholes running this operation that we're coming for all of them.* That's the only reason he's alive. That should knock this shit off down here for a good long while. The Canadian broad has no idea what the hell just happened and just looks shell-shocked. The other passengers are smiling, laughing, shaking my hand, making fun of the dead and I'm like "get the fuck going c'mon!"

Baldy rips out as fast as that big piece of shit bus will go, and I've got a bandana wrapped around my face now, holding the AK. Just as the big bus disappears the purple Jeep turns the corner, pulls in and sees only me, guns it and starts to turn around while I unload. No skill required here—it's an AK, fully-loaded. *I checked.* The car veers sharply right, toward me! Then slows, and finally rolls through the pull-off and smashes the nose into a tree. Not a good plan on my part, I guess. But not too much front-end damage. All of the right side windows are blown-out, the nose dented, radiator's leaking a little. Dead driver, not too much blood. No sweat, I ride with the windows down, and all the cars down here are beat to shit anyway! I drag all 5 bodies into the trees so the coyotes, jackals, leopards, necromancers and whatever the hell else they have down there will eat them. *I keep one of the 9mm's as a souvenir.*

So what did you think? Killing a fly with a sledgehammer? Too violent for your tastes? *Am I just a lawless asshole criminal with no regard for human life?* Well, some of that is true. But lawlessness is just that. So are bad guys. Welcome to life after the Fall-

What you've just read can be representative of how we go about planning our operations in the next life. All of the elements are the same, although I would assert that the road to Leon' was more dangerous than anything we might run into during any Ops we run in the next life. Let's break that last little episode down a bit:

<u>Objective</u>—Stop the explosion of kidnapping and rapes along a major Nicaraguan highway. Find out who's responsible.

<u>Reconnaissance</u>—My first ride from Managua to Leon'. Notice I observed and understood the demographics, the background, the interaction, timing, things that stood out from the rest. Witnessed the action. Language, voices, their level of professionalism, their timing, equipment, etc. Remember what I said about this part being the most dangerous? I could have easily been taken out here; I had no idea what I was getting into-

<u>Identifying Multiple Targets of Opportunity</u>—in this case the targets were the Savvys, the bus driver and the Contras.

<u>Qualifying Each Opportunity</u>—That was easy. The bad guys all played the same part on the second ride. They were for real.

Target Selection—In this case I opted for the Savvy's and the Contras. They were the executors of their own plans. The bus driver was a well-paid stooge.

Goals For Each Target—*Death*. This was not about vengeance. Or revenge (although that little prick got what he deserved after smashing my face). Death is the language they speak. They also understand the universal sign language, *Money*, but I wasn't communicating that way on that day—Their leaders got the message.

Planning The Operation—This is always one of the fun parts. I need to take out the two Contra boys in order to send a message; The Savvy boys are the local connection, and they are in my way, so they need to be removed. The bus driver is the key to delivering the message. *Step 1, turn the bus driver*—as he is the mainstay, and just a paid tool, he's easy to compromise. Hence the photos of his daughter. "We" never really had her, of course, that was just a ruse. Deception is the primary weapon of Intelligence operatives. Baldy didn't know that, however, as the photo was a day old and he knew it, and the fact that I blew the Savvys' brains out made him a true believer. *Step 2—neutralize the Savvys*. Well, I call them savvy for a reason; they were. So I figured I'd have to kill them too. *Collateral damage*. Positioning was key here, and, of course the element of surprise. I sat directly behind one of them, easy first kill. The second would be a little harder, but the shock and surprise of a sudden firefight gets to everyone, especially when it starts with some little gay guy. I didn't think about the window, though. *Shit Happens!* OK so now I have to figure out how to take out the Contras, in a very short window of time. I'll admit to winging this a little, but I knew I would maneuver into position for the right shots, I just didn't know which first, or when. The blown-out bus window gave me away, but also gave me the opportunity to take out the AK. The rest was easy. Plug the little snot-nosed kid, get the bus out of there, hijack the Jeep Commander so I could get the hell out of there. Again, this was a surprise to all of them, so it was easy. *Shit Happens! This time it happened to them!*

Staging The Order Of Operations—Usually this applies when running multiple Ops, but it applies here as well. There were multiple targets, of different threat levels, all to be addressed at different times. The Savvy's were pros, and dangerous. *First up, first out*—Baldy the bus driver was way up front, probably not a threat with a handgun, and just a tool anyway, so *Next*. That leaves the Contras. Sometimes the staging just unfolds. Serendipity gave me the opportunity to take out my biggest threat. *Luck happens too!*

Implementation—Well, it's just that. You read the story, can understand the planning outlined above, this is just the Execution of the Plan. The Psychology was in making Baldy think we had his daughter, blowing the Savvys up was intimidation, you get the rest—all it takes is commitment. And balls. You wouldn't be doing any of this if you possessed neither.

Post-Operation Follow-Up—Sometimes things need a change-up, so I paid some kid and his abuelita to ride the bus every week for a month. My luck and disguises were running out, and I wasn't taking chances on not having anyone waiting for me. As I mentioned earlier, this is the other most dangerous time. But nothing was happening. Their operations stopped dead cold. If they hadn't stopped I would have come back down and throttled Baldy a little harder, to dig deeper into the operation. But then that becomes a bigger investigation, you have to rope in more guys, it gets more attention, whaa whaa whaa. *And I would have wanted more money!* But they had gotten the message. *Sometimes this shit actually works.*

Usually I take a vacation after one of the little operations. Something to wash the stench and blood from my head and hands. I recommend that you do as well. Enjoy the fruits of your labor. The spoils of victory. Otherwise, why the Hell else would you be doing anything like this after the Fall? For exercise? Are you crazy? Listen up again: The world is going to suck worse than you can ever imagine if civilization ever really does disintegrate. *Take in the good moments whenever you can, as there won't be too many of them.*

In this case I went skiing up at Jackson Hole. One of my favorite spots. Cold, fresh air. Smells and feels clean. Well-heeled business types and their attractive, college-educated wives. Wearing fur! About as far away as you can get from Nicaragua. I needed that just about then. My bosses at the bank thought I was on the road visiting clients. Yeah, well, I was making *a lot* of money for them, so they really didn't keep close tabs. After all that just went down, I really didn't give a shit anyway, and my face was still a little bruised and swollen . . .

Ok so let's apply these lessons real time . . .

CHAPTER 7

Taking Out a Lightly Defended Farm

Let's go take down a well-stocked, lightly-defended farm, say, in Mexico, circa 1985. Of course there are no cell phones, but there are cars—We'll cut them some slack and pretend second-generation night vision was invented. This is a hypothetical, but loosely based on a real operation. I wrote it up as one of my True Personal Stories, but let's do it piece by piece, together, so you can get an understanding as to how this all unfolds.

In this case as we're starting with a target already identified and qualified, so we'll start with Recon.

Reconnaissance is a personal thing. Everybody trained in it in some way shape or form has his own preferences as to what to look for, how to look for it, what is important, what is less so, timing, numbers, etc., etc. I consider reconnaissance to be the difference between life and death. I was trained in both military style and intelligence style reconnaissance. They are both similar, of course, but have some prominent and some other, more subtle distinctions. Usually I'm working on my own or in a very small group. I have a very specific objective. I need to get into a place, get out of a place, or take something or someone from a place. Some military objectives are the same, but many times they are looking to move through an area, retreat from an area, take possession of an area, or "plow the road" so to speak. They can also afford to take casualties while conducting recon. I cannot. My style has more in common with SEAL or Marine Force Recon style. They have very similar objectives to mine, and cannot afford casualties either. They too, usually only get one shot at it.

So in this case here I'm looking specifically to find out:

1. Is there anything on this ranch worth having?
2. Is there anything on this ranch worth getting shot at for?
3. How well defended is it?
4. Are there professional military onsite?
5. Does the terrain harm or help?
6. Will the ranch burn if necessary?
7. Can we get close enough easily enough?
8. Can we get close enough and remain undetected?

Ok so first we get in as close as we think we can safely get without being detected. Remember in an earlier chapter I discussed taking out your enemy from as far away as possible? The same thing applies to initial Recon. See what you can see from as far away as possible at first. If not, you may unknowingly get too close and move inside a perimeter that you need to detect, being *outside* of it. I can't stress this enough. Especially if you have the unfortunate luck of running up against SEALs or Green Berets. *They know the perimeter!* That means time in the field. A lot of it. Mostly on your belly, or in some other contorted position that will make you extremely uncomfortable. You might get very hot. You might get very cold. You might want to quit. But sooner or later, you will discover something important, maybe that one little thing that makes the operation a GO, maybe a NO GO, or the difference between life and death. So suck it up. Glass the place for hours. See what's out there. Stay with it through the night. Back off, back out. Come back again in a day or two, Repeat. Then make your decision.

In this specific case, our four days of Recon revealed lots of food, a fresh water supply, and weapons (which usually means ammo) as well. *This is a fabulous target!* Occupying the ranch are at least three men and three women, with 4 or 5 kids as well. It is situated out in the open, a big, 2-storey stuccoed main ranch house, a big-ass wood barn, and a metal pole-house garage. It's probably 75 meters to the short scrub from the main house, then another 25 yards to the tree line. It's set in a tiny valley with scrub oak hills running up a couple of hundred yards behind it, and only one way in and out—a mile long loose dirt road, along which runs the power and phone lines. It's obviously exposed, but we still shouldn't get too close in the daytime. Two visible Jeep Wranglers and one Cherokee out front, always a possibility there's another one in the garage. We walked concentric decreasing circles about a mile out and moving in, looking for any sign of professional (military) activity or preparations, things like lots of tracks back and forth to covered shooting positions, escape routes, booby traps, tripwires, dead-end trail trap points, etc. We found none, which leads us to believe there's no ex-military here. *Do you see the kinds of things you need to look for?*

Our <u>Goal</u> is to get the bulk of the food, and any ammo we might need.

First Move, Psychological Warfare — About a mile up the road, middle of the afternoon, we cut the power and phone lines. They will come out and take a look, of course, and easily find that they've been intentionally cut, as we will leave them clearly dangling. *They know they have trouble.* They hightail it back to the ranch after repairing the lines, too late to leave — Later that night, under the cover of darkness, we crawl into the scrub 75 meters from the main house. On a piece of paper we have written a proper note outlining our demands — some amount of food, ammo, etc., and telling them to deliver it out to the scrub line in the morning. We request that they also return any arrows as well. We ask if they would just give it up politely, in which case we will go away, and they will suffer no harm. We roll this message up and wrap it around the arrow of our crossbow. We fire it off into the front door of the house, *then leave.* If the crack of the arrow into the door wakes them up, great. If not, they'll find it in the morning.

Ok so now we are at home (base camp, wherever that is on that day), enjoying the weather, the scenery, swimming in the creek, or enjoying a good meal. This is in stark contrast to the residents of the farm, having heard the crack of the arrow into the door last night, read the note and haven't slept a wink or relaxed since they found their wires cut! We spend the rest of the afternoon doing recon around another ranch, about ten miles in the opposite direction —

Ranch #2 is a little bit tougher task, as there's less cover, with the thin scrub ending about 100 yards from the main house. This main house is also two storeys tall, with all of the windows on the first floor boarded up in plywood. It's covered in an old-style wood batten-board brown siding. *Yay!* Front door dead center. Kitchen door, single wood panel, left side back. Only two doors. Strong-looking tin sheet roof. To the right, a really large, tall, gorgeous gray weathered wood barn angled nicely towards the main house, about fifty yards away, fifty feet across. About five acres fenced in behind the barn, five horses in view. A Paint, two Chestnuts, some blacks, maybe more in the barn. The door's wide open. This is a big, beautiful place. One I might like to keep for a while! An older, brown Ford F-150 and one newer Land Rover Defender parked on a gravel sway in between the two buildings. *That Defender is a yellow beauty! Maybe we'll take her for a ride*! One long, dirt road in, about five miles from the main highway (a relative term, as it's paved, that's all). Of course the phone and power lines are strung haphazardly along it.

Ranch #2—First Move, Psychological Warfare—We cut the lines just for the Hell of it. Let them know somebody's around-

That night we fire an arrow into the front door of Ranch #2, outlining demands similar to those made of the first ranch, etc., etc., in addition to psych war this is also <u>Staging</u>. When we finish with Ranch #1 we'll start Recon on #3 then finish-up this current Ranch #2. Remember, *this is a business. We need to keep it running.* We go back home and have a few cocktails, then get a good night's sleep while the folks at Ranch #2 are scared shitless and haven't relaxed since they lost power and phone earlier that day and won't sleep a wink tonight!

Two days later we show up at Ranch #1 again. No food, ammo or anything is left in the designated spot for us. They have guys with AR-15's peeking out the second floor windows. Typical. And expected. But it's been 2 days, and they're tired, on edge, getting on each other's nerves. They've kept the kids inside the whole time. *That alone would make ME give it up!* The women have been very vocal in expressing their fear. Lots of crying. They're all starting to feel it now.

Second Move, Intimidation—On that visit, from cover, we unload into the tires and radiators of the SUV's. Fire off another arrow into the door with another note that says "Don't be silly, this will just get worse." Then we go home, again. But first, we check a wide circle around the ranch looking for tracks and/or other sign, in case they have some tough guys *scouting us*—This is critical, though, as a lot of tracks or sign tells us maybe they're thinking defensively, or guarding the perimeter, or setting up defensive spots outside the ranch. But we find nothing, except big coyote tracks.

The next night we head back to Ranch #2—

Third Move, Attack Prep—Back at Ranch 1, on the fourth night, we approach quietly, looking through the night vision goggles. We have the dogs with us. Before we get too close, we toss a tennis ball out ahead of us, and the border collies go chasing it. They'll flush out anyone in hiding or will set off any booby-traps that might have been placed since we were last there.

We don't care if they know we're out there or not, we just don't want to get tagged by some homemade improvised crap. Border collies are really goddamned smart, and I'd hate to lose one, but they are an extremely effective flush mechanism. Just throw a tennis ball. We do this a few times, covering a wide area between the ranch and us. It's all clear. But it's possible that the folks at the ranch heard us, or we tripped a wire, whatever, and they're watching us from somewhere in or around the house. I don't give a shit.

Fourth Move, Attack—I don the Level III body armor, dump the AK and bring the Walther, along with a book of matches and three Molotov cocktails. I'm exposed here if anyone in the house has a Starlight scope or early laser targeting system. If a shot is fired though, our guys in the trees will unload on the source and keep up a barrage. I run like hell toward the barn, (try hitting me on the run at night with a Starlight scope, nope!) light and launch one onto the roof, and two into the big front doors. The flames catch hold of the wood siding. There are three horses in the barn, so I leave the door ajar. *I like horses.* I turn and get ready to sprint back . . .

Well, you can imagine what's going on inside the main ranch house right about now. The women are probably just about at the breaking point. The men were waiting for something to happen and, well, damn, this is it! They opt to let the barn burn down (shame on them, the horses are in there), as they can't operate in darkness, and are scared we might be lurking about. *I never lurk. It's boring.* The kids are screaming freaking out because the barn's now on fire and they think the horses are in there. I can actually hear them. But everyone is still sitting tight inside. Figures. *Sheep!*

Ok I'm not perfect, just pretty damned good! But I missed something important during my initial Recon. The dog. *Beast* is more like it. I had a second chance at it when I saw the big coyote tracks. They were actually *dog* tracks. Well, *Shit Happens!* A big, *really big* German Shepherd is now about 30 yards out and pounding toward me at full speed. He's deadly silent and I only see him because his great big Little Red Riding Hood white teeth caught a glint of the barn fire. *Christ, he got the drop on me! A fucking dog!* Now, I know we've already discussed Handguns in an earlier section, but I neglected to mention that it's pretty damn hard to take out a dog at close range coming at you full speed. It has a very small silhouette. *Really!* I turn and with two hands gripping the Walther BAMBAMBAMBAMBAMBAMBAM empty the magazine into the dog. And the ground. And the air around him. I nailed him though, but only twice, in the snout and chest. That was enough, of course. He drops dead about 10 feet in front of me and his momentum slides him right up to my boots. At least 90lbs. God-DAMN he would have left a mark. *WHEW!* OK I hightail it back to the treeline and head home again. Mission accomplished. Their barn's on fire, they think their horses are dead, they heard gunfire, their dog hasn't come back, WAH WAH WAH I can hear the women crying kids screaming stick a fork in this place. They're done . . .

Fifth Move, Assessment—This is when we decide if we want to escalate or not—We show up the next afternoon, and right in front of the shrub line is a big cache of food cans, a few boxes of 9mm ammo, a few boxes of 7.62, and my two arrows. We have enough water, so this looks like a pretty good haul. *We'll have to make a couple of trips!* We start firing the 30-30 into the air over the ranch, and gather up the food and ammo under the covering fire. We locate the horses on the way back out and take the strongest-looking one with us. Chestnut mare. Beautiful. *Another souvenir.* Maybe we can buy a lottery ticket and get a Slurpee on the last trip!

A few hours later, after we've got it all stashed safely away, I hike back on over and lob another arrow into the front door. This time the note reads:

Thanks for the stuff. I left you two horses, sorry about the dog.
See you next year-
Kilkenny

That was pretty goddamned easy, don't you think? Sure was! At first they tried playing it smart by staying tight and hunkering down, though that never works with my approach. They made a mistake with the dog, as they should have kept him tight also, although he almost put the bite on me. Keep the dog for when you really need it. I'm going to beat you from within anyway—They were probably killing themselves in that house for 5 days worrying about these invisible marauders, while we ate well, kicked back, had a few beers, a lot of laughs, were working on and planning other operations, and slept soundly at night.

OK Kilkenny, any idiot could have done what you did. They didn't even put up a fight!

Correct, of course. But I didn't know if they would or wouldn't. I'm the one that took the risk. And even though it turned out to be as easy as it gets, *Shit Happens* and in this case it was the dog, and he almost got me. He could have torn me up pretty damn good. Then I would have had to deal with fixing my arm or leg, or both, fighting infection, pain meds, etc. Remember, after the Fall any one of these things can result in your immediate termination.

That said, I take your premise and say ok we'll step it up on ourselves a little, and show you what happened at Ranch #2, which was very well defended. Fair?

CHAPTER 8

Taking Out A Well-Defended Ranch

Okay, so in the last chapter while taking out Ranch #1 we had also begun our initial work on Ranch #2, and began scouting around for our future targets. *Remember, this is a business! We need to keep it moving.* So here we will pick up our activities regarding a more heavily defended target:

Ranch #2—*Second Move, Intimidation*—During our second visit to the house, four nights out, they unloaded on us. I tossed the ball twice, then got clipped on my vest high on the right shoulder, glanced off. *Great target acquisition! This guy's a pro!* Pretty goddamned loud, too, all of which tells me it was probably the NATO round from an M-16. I didn't take it personally, of course. But it still pissed me off! We had the goggles but they did too, apparently, and whomever probably put the little red laser dot on my chest about 100 yards out, which they could see, of course, with their night vision goggles or Starlight scope. It sounds easy, but it's not easy to do if you haven't practiced it, so the guy that tagged me is ex-military. A real pro, probably a Marine, as they use that type of nighttime targeting system. The shot came from the main ranch house, and I think if it were SEAL or Green Beret they would have hit me from cover outside. Which leaves me with an either-or: *EITHER* he's the *ONLY* ex-military guy in there, *OR* other SEALs or Green Berets are out and around us now. In the darkness it was easy to see where the shot came from, so my guys unloaded and silenced that position. Probably no casualties. This is the defining moment, though, as the other guys, my guys, have exposed themselves—If SEALs are in the woods now, my guys are probably toast—***This is why we do Recon!*** We didn't get the impression that there was any SEAL or Green Beret presence around the place. How can I tell? By their defenses. None, except for having all of the first floor windows covered in plywood. *A cocktail will light them up really well.* No fence, wire, or dogs. We saw no human tracks around the place on our second day there. Special Ops guys *ALWAYS* watch the perimeter, seek escape routes, create covered shooting positions, etc. There was nothing out there even remotely indicating anything like that. No big coyote tracks either! ***Again, are you understanding the kinds of things you need to find during Recon?*** And on our way in that night, we sent the border collies ahead as usual and they sprung no booby traps or came upon anyone hiding out. It wasn't until I tossed the ball that I got locked-on by the guy at the ranch. We're probably safe, but I give the signal to retreat anyway. *Stealthily.* Let them think they've won, while we go home, have a drink, get a good night's sleep. Ok, so *Intimidation* didn't quite go as planned. Oh well . . . Get out the blue paint. We'll alter the plan in the morning. But they'll be up all night, nervous and sweating, until we show up again. *And we will.*

Remember now, the timeline. We've just finished up the operation at Ranch #1, so we're pretty fat and happy. The next day we decide to scout out our next few targets while we let Ranch #2 simmer a little bit. They have no idea if they've killed one of us, if we're gone for good, coming back, whatever. There were three women on the place, no kids, but I'm sure whatever men they have are hearing it from the gals right now. *As they should.* On the second day after their counter attack we start drawing up the new plan. When we hit them again it will have been three full days later, a full week after our initial contact and I'm sure they're exhausted, angry and irritable. *Perfect!*

When you're out on your own on a field op in the intelligence business, you quickly figure out that the ground moves out from under you, the weather forecast goes from sunny and 65 to snow in about an hour and just generally the circumstances and the rules are always in a state of flux. One of the reasons I was so successful (read: still alive) is that I am *the best* at improvisation. Almost MacGyver-like. I can build a Tesla from a golf cart, a flashlight and duct tape. *I'm really that good!* No offense to Elon Musk, who is clearly a genius-

So all of us after the Fall, especially Marauders, need to get really good at this. Things change, setbacks occur, Murphy raises his ugly head—*Shit Happens!* So we constantly need to adapt, change our plan, maybe even our objective. Take what the defense gives us. *Use Blue!* So with this in mind, we've altered the plan for taking out Ranch #2. They've proven they can be formidable, have taken a stand against us (at least for now) and are forcing us to work harder and longer at getting what we want.

Time out right now—Do we want to go ahead with our takedown of this ranch, knowing there's going to be shooting, fire and maybe somebody gets killed? Do we even need anything from this ranch? We were pretty successful on our last haul, we have lots of supplies from other hauls, and our prospects look pretty damn good. At Ranch #2 they have at least one ex-Marine who is a pretty good shot, willing to engage and who nicked me in the shoulder of my vest (which actually hurts pretty bad right now, as even though the round glanced off, I've got a pretty goddamned deep bruise on the top of my shoulder from it). So we should probably back off and find easier pickin's-

Not! Hell No—These guys wanna tussle a little bit, well ok then! This is the fun stuff sometimes. We don't know how it will turn out, but we're way better than these guys, so we're gonna go take 'em down!

Ranch #2—*Third Move, Attack Prep*—We stage another thorough daytime Recon inside a wide circular perimeter, as before, looking for tracks, covered positions, escape routes, any reasonable signs of activity. And dog tracks. Nothing. So far, so good—I continue to believe these are not special ops guys. Just for good measure though, we keep two guys watching on opposite corners of the main ranch house (so we can see all four sides), all during the daylight hours. I'm one of them. It's a pain in the ass, and horrifically boring. The danger here, of course, is that we nod off and miss something. It's hot, there's no breeze, there's bugs bleeding and feeding on us, and there are scorpions around. It sucks, but Hell this is what we get paid for!

Nothing. And nothing. More nothing. Jesus Christ these guys are idiots. We've been at them on and off for about a week, their nerves must be shot, they can't be sleeping well, the women must be ripping the men, it should be miserable in there! So why am I so freakin' miserable out here in the scrub? *Because I'm out here in the scrub! For hours! Watching nothing!* C'mon guys, *DO SOMETHING*. Anything! Please make me believe I actually needed to put in all of this effort for Christ's sake, and that it wasn't as easy as firing off a few rounds at the house. *Dammit!*

And just when you think it's safe to go back in the water, Boom! CRACKCRACKCRACKCRACKCRACKCRACKCRACK CRACK SUPPRESSING FIRE FROM TWO SECOND FLOOR WINDOWS DUST AND LEAD DANCING UP ALL AROUND US WAIT WAIT DON'T MOVE !! There's a guy racing from around the back of the house toward the barn, empty-handed. The fire stops when he reaches it. *Jesus Fucking Christ.*

Okay, so while I was whining a little bit they showed that they're a little bit smarter, or more ballsy, than I was starting to give them credit for. That laydown wasn't directed at us, though, it was directed at *the potential* of us—They don't know if we're out here or not. Maybe they do this all the time. This was our first daytime stakeout of this ranch, so, whatever. Clearly they need stuff from the barn. Maybe the guys need toilet paper because their asses are getting so chewed!

About five minutes later the same guy comes running, stumbling fumbling from the barn with about 8 gallons of water! SHIT! SLAM!! WE ARE FACE DOWN AS THE FIRE COMES ROARING BACK OUR WAY FROM THE RANCH AGAIN A FULL THIRTY SECONDS OR LONGER AND I'M

SURE THE GUY IS BACK INSIDE. We can smell the acrid powder, mixed with the dust kicked up from the scrub. It's clogging my nose and burning my eyeballs. *Crap! This is getting to be a real pain in the ass! Ok, I'm getting really cranky now!*

It's smoky, dusty, the M-16's are tucked back inside the windows. Perfect time to get the hell out and get back home. We got all the information we needed for now. *Attack prep successful,* though a little rougher than we thought. I give the signal and we head out-

Okay, so as we're heading back, anticipating the next move in our plan, let's look at what we derived from our Recon today:

1. *They don't leave the house much, if at all*—No tracks, covered shooting positions, outside defensive positions, blinds, or any kind of real activity around the ranch. No dog tracks. Nobody's gonna spring up from under the ground and slit our throats, nor are we going to get conked in the head by a .22LR from somewhere outside of the main ranch house.
2. *They're still operating on high alert*—The fact that they're laying down suppression means they're worried, cautious, expecting us. Which is good news, as they're very likely physically and psychologically exhausted. This makes them prone to mistakes, and prone to quitting.
3. *They've decided to hole-up*—Perfect! I was hoping these guys would grow some stones, so I could at least justify all the bullshit we've put up with!

4. *They keep a lot of supplies in the Barn.* This is a big boo-boo of course. It's kind of tough to get your supplies when you're under siege and they're in a different building! Now, maybe they've been running out there like they did today a little bit here and there, trying to load up, but if they're as "prepped" as I think they are, there's still a lot more valuable stuff in the Barn.
5. *They've got at least two good shooters*—Well that was kind of obvious today! I'm still betting only one Marine, though. Nevertheless, two to worry about.
6. *I did not see this but just realized it* . . . the 4wheelers are gone!—Crap, I told you that Recon gets so boring that you can miss things. We didn't nod off, but nothing looked out of place because nothing was there! I'm sure they moved them into the garage or the barn. This will change my plan a little, *again*.

Ok, back at base camp we're preparing for tonight's activities. We're going right back at them now, no wasting time. Our MO up to this point has been longer periods of waiting, like Chinese Water Torture on the guys at the ranch, while we kick back a little and go scouting out new targets. Not now. Ranch #3 will have to wait. It's time.

Ranch #2—*Fourth Move, Attack*—With the dogs tied-up back at base camp, we take the horses and head out. As we get inside 300 yards of the ranch house, we start putting on our own M-16 show, loud and long into the scrub ahead of us as we move in on the ranch. *"C'mon boys, let's plow the road!"* They're on alert now at the ranch, but surely have their heads tucked safely inside. I'm sure they'll respond when we let up—I HATE wasting ammo, but I'm betting they've got a big cache on the property here. And besides, I like the plan.

We get to about 150 yards out, hold up, seek cover behind the skinny trees, and cease fire. And wait. Nothing! Damn! I was hoping they would immediately return fire, but they don't. *Pros!* We're going to have to encourage them!

Ok, so I don the body armor, take a fully-saddled paint and start moving slowly, quietly through the treeline, into the scrub. The paint is planted firmly between the ranch house and me. I start the horse galloping, and dive into the scrub as a couple of shots from an M-16 at the house ring out—I don't know if the horse is hit or not, but it trots toward the house, then about a hundred yards out cuts away sharply left, stirrups and saddle strings flopping limply against her sides as she trots away. No more fire from the house. *Excellent!*

I yell "let's go" and then, as I was hoping, a laydown of suppressing fire erupts from the ranch house. *Perfect!* We wait for the barrage to end, then I grab the fully-saddled big chestnut mare from Ranch #1, and keeping her, also, firmly placed between the ranch house and me, start her trotting out toward the house as well. This time I am running along side her.

I don't know if we fooled them or not, but I always hope that the riderless, fully-saddled horse trick works. Sometimes yes, sometimes no. We're about 50 yards from the garage now, still no fire from the ranch. *Whew! These guys really are* CRACK

CRACK CRACK CRACKCRACKCRACK about 25 yards out they're firing again I know the horse is hit, but the .22LR doesn't work on a horse the way it does on a man, so she bolts hard I'm sprinting alongside and dive safely up along the side of the pole garage, and the paint keeps galloping off . . .

What assholes! They shot a perfectly good horse! Well, not really. If it were me, I would have shot that big chestnut as soon as she popped out of the scrub. But that's just me. The military-trained mind thinks a bit differently. A riderless horse isn't a typical acquired target, so when presented, the brain freezes for a second or so. I'm sure the guy in the house hesitated, and it was long enough for me to get where I needed to be. Like I said, I'd have shot her in the head when she first popped up.

I'm betting they saw me, but it doesn't matter. I slip through one of the two side by side sliding windows on the barn wall away from the house. So far, so good. No fire from the house. If somebody comes running my way he'll get cut down by my boys in the trees. If they send someone out back and around the compound the long way, well, I'm always ready but I'll probably be gone by then.

The F-150 is parked there facing the front of the big garage door. I slide over and peek in—it's an automatic, *Perfect Again!* Makes things a lot easier. It's locked, I smash the passenger window with the rifle butt. Don't want *my* butt to get any glass in it. This, of course, is an old F-150, and it couldn't be any easier to hotwire. Oh, I forgot to mention this in an earlier chapter. *Learn how to hotwire a car.* Just in case. Like for right now!

Well, as we expected, this was a well-prepped ranch. Cans of gasoline and kerosene of all sizes run along the back wall. The back of the F-150 is empty, but I douse the entire vehicle in gasoline anyway. I hotwire the ignition, and the F-150 is ready to go! I open the big garage door and then my guys start laying down fire on the ranch house, I drive out as fast as I can maneuver and turn left around the side of the barn, make a big U-turn and stop. I've got the Molotov cocktail ready. I plunk one of those big old round, green kerosene cans down on the accelerator, put it in drive, foot hard on the brake until we turn the corner. She's pointed straight at the ranch house front door now, I jump out the passenger side in to the garage as we blow by and as the suppression starts up again, light the cocktail, toss it into the bed and that truck now BOOOMPH!!! *EXPLODES* into flames and starts picking up speed then SMASH*CRASHES* right up the short porch *SLAM* through the front of the house. Just like we planned it! The entire hood is sticking into the front room of the house, and the flames have now caught the front wall of the ranch. I can hear screaming on the inside, all kinds of chaos, but they get a fire extinguisher on the truck, and put the front end out. Good for them. Unfortunately their house is catching fire. They will have to come outside to stop that.

Just then the barrel of an M-16 jabs out the window! *But it's got a white towel hanging off it.* "Ok!" I yell. "You can come out and put out the fire." They send one of the women out with an extinguisher. Nice move. They think we won't shoot an unarmed woman. They're correct. *Not from this distance.* She does a damn fine job, and some of the others are putting it out on the inside as well. Everything quiets down pretty quickly. We're still in cover, so I yell out "Ok, do we have to go to round 2?"

"What do you want?" somebody yells back.

"Food! Lots of it! And 5000 rounds of ammo. 9mm, 22LR, 30.30, a mix" I casually reply.

"We only have 5000 rounds left!"

"Bullshit!" I yell. "There's an ammo locker in that garage that's pretty goddamn heavy. 5000!"

I saw the box but didn't give it a thought. Would they be that stupid to leave ammo in that garage?

"OK" comes the reply.

Well yes, I guess they would be that stupid. *I love Preppers!*

I'll spare you the rest of the back and forth, as you can probably figure it out. We haul out about two months of food, a couple of six-packs and a bottle of Jack! The raid on this place was worth it just for the Jack! Mission accomplished, and *GodDamn* that was fun!

So what did you think about that one? A little too daring for you? A little too crazy? Well, actually, it was neither. It was very well-planned. Our Recon was really well done. We paid attention to detail. We used blue. Got creative. Showed balls. If you can't do any of this stuff, close the book now and go back to growing stuff in your Doomsday Prepper Garden-

If we didn't have horses we would have conjured up a different plan. Probably one that would have hurt the ranchers more, probably a little more violent—Don't have dogs you can use to flush? Well then you have to spend a Hell of a lot more time in Recon, keeping a guy stationed on watch 24/7, in the scrub or trees or whatever instead, until you make your move. *Adapt* to the situation, take what the defense gives you, and go be MacGyver when you have to. Again, if you can't do *any* of this then you probably can't grow turnips either!

Not enough for you? Still think we're robbing the cradle or taking candy from babies? Are you challenging us to go after the big boys, maybe a prepper colony that's got some military guys, maybe a SEAL or Green Beret or two? Well usually I don't rise to take anyone's bait. I go fishin' where I want and when I choose to. And as I've said before, there are so many easy idiot doomsday prepper targets out there why in my right mind would I take on a whole colony, some of whom are ex-military, with only four guys?

Because I can!

Let's face it—after the fall of civilization it's going to be pretty damn boring. I'm not going to be able to sit around, watch the news, criticize the current administration, complain about America's role in world affairs, annoy everyone around me and threaten to write a book. I won't be able to call every important play as I'm watching Monday Night Football, draft a national champion fantasy football team, or go to Vegas. Vegas! And women, or lack thereof for Christ's sake, what the hell am I going to do about that! Life will truly suck.

So, then, I guess from time to time the thing that will keep *me* going (or get me killed) in the next life will be *The Rush*. That's the reason I'll take on the big boys. It's a big operation, takes a long time, but it's really a *huge rush* and a whole bunch of fun. If you live, of course.

Many people have said "you never feel so alive as when you're close to death." Well, that's a bunch of shit. When I've been close to death I didn't smell any flowers, catch the taste of wild grasses on the breeze, notice how beautiful the blue sky is, thought everything's wonderful or any of that crap! I've usually smelled gunpowder, oil, the dirt that my face is smashed down in, somebody's ass if my head's buried in it fighting to the death, tasted blood in my mouth, the seawater I'm choking on as I'm drowning and have seen extremely clearly, the sunlight, *glinting off the instrument of my death,* a 9mm or a big blade or some guy 6'4 250, all the while thinking 'Not now dammit not now dammit goddammit not now!' So trust me, when you're very close to death, it's extremely stressful. And it completely sucks.

Chasing death, on the other hand, is a *whole* different thing. Ask Everest guides, or base jumpers. It's the Adrenaline, the Risk, the Rush. We've all chased death at times, hoping never to actually catch it. The thrill of the chase is more important to so many of us in this current life, and at least for me, it might be one of the only two exciting things left for me in the next life as well (finding sex would be the other one). I fully expect, as well, that I will one day chase and ultimately catch, Death. Hence my willingness to take on the ultimate challenge. The

KILKENNY

Colony, 50 people, a couple of SEALs, lots of shooters. And women. *Souvenirs, maybe?*

Before we start, in keeping with my personal style and the spirit of this book, let's go back again and re-live a situation from my past that actually brought me the closest to peeing my pants. Literally. This was the most scared I have ever been. Hopefully my experience will help you all when faced with similar, maybe ambiguous circumstances, and help you determine a decision-making process to deal with it. And to teach you to always, *always*—stay cool.

CHAPTER 9

The Belly of the Sexy Beast

They called him Chupacabra, like the mysterious, mythical, dog-like wolf-like creature that mutilates its prey and bleeds it dry, scattering bloody, mutilated bodies and body parts about like a grizzly scattering trash out of a dumpster. Nowadays there is evidence that it may actually exist, but for years in Latin America they've feared the sheer ferocity, destructive power and rabid insanity of this mystical creature like no other . . .

Chupacabra was an enforcer in the army of Pablo Escobar. "Enforcer" being the polite, politically correct term we use today instead of Assassin. As an Enforcer, *he is the most savage, blood-hungry-mutilation-obsessed-horror-inducing creature I have ever encountered.* He scares the total shit out of me, to this day, even though I was notified by our government years ago that he had been killed by his own crew. I never completely bought it, though, I mean, really, you don't think that Pablo Escobar died in that shootout in 93' either, do you? The U.S. and Colombia together "arranged" many such deaths in wild-west type shootouts down there, in order to restore some faith to the Colombian people, that their government could actually get something done, and might actually find a way to end the never-ending civil war down there. The drug lords were winning, after all. *It was completely out of control!* They had no choice but to stage these things. Pablo Escobar now lives in Spain. No shit. Don't believe it? Then I suppose you think that Lee Harvey Oswald acted alone, as well.

We've all heard something like "That guy would kill his own mother." Well, Chupacabra did. Really. Found her in bed with a guy other than his long-dead father. He was sixteen. I also had the "pleasure" of an invite to the notorious Colombian Gladiator Ring out in the Colombian countryside northwest of Bogota' during which I watched this maniac, about 6'1, 210lbs, fight three guys to the death. As he's literally punching in one guy's skull he gets shanked really hard from behind in the right kidney. Unimpeded, he finishes crushing that poor rival soldier's skull so hard that the eyeballs pop out, then gets shanked again! He turns and grabs the throat of his attacker and literally rips it out! Holding the guy up by his scalp with his right hand and with his left strikes with lightning force, crushing the windpipe, grabbing and pulling it back out almost effortlessly with *skin, muscle, cartilage, esophagus, blood* pouring right out with it. I've never seen such savage, brute force. I'm not squeamish by any means, and I've also made a few guys leak brains, but this almost made me vomit. Blood is spewing everywhere, all over us spectators as well. I guess I got a little white in the face, and the Colombians noticed, but that one little bit of true humanity I still held onto betrayed me as a "regular" guy. If I was so steely-eyed badass right then they might have thought "soldier." Chupacabra walks away. They drove him 200 miles to a hospital in Bogota, then after a few days he's on a G4 to Miami for surgical repair work. I can't believe he survived. *Thrived!*

One of his cute little quirks was peeling the skin off of captured rival cartel soldiers while they were still alive, and making soup out of it. The other captives were forced to eat the soup made from their comrades (and the old bones of other rival soldiers) before *they* became soup. The soup also contained some of their testicles, some that Chupacabra would rip off by hand, and an eyeball or two he would plunk out with his fingers. *All while his captives were still alive!* You watched him make soup, then ate soup, *then became soup.* When there was nobody left to eat the soup, he would finish it himself. A sick, twisted, sadistic fuck.

So flash forward again a couple of years—Now I'm in that very same G4, on the way to Miami from Bogota' as well. Chupacabra is sitting directly across the table from me, staring into my eyes as if he couldn't wait to taste them . . .

The last two months had gone very, very well. I'd finally been accepted and approved as one of the Cartel's money launderers. This, of course, *is huge,* as now we can now begin to follow the money. I was at the Tequendama Hotel in Bogota' to tie up the details. Right now, right here, being a contract guy was the only way to crack these guys. I was vetted top to bottom, upways and sideways, so much so that even some legitimate financing deals I had arranged for the bank years ago back in the U.S. were utterly scrutinized by this gang. It was tight, I was legit. Truth is, *I really was an international banker. I did a lot of deals. Laid out a lot of money. Had lots of contacts and lots of references. Everybody liked doing business with me. Life had been really, really good!* The Agency paid me to do stuff, of course, but basically I worked for myself. I'd been cashing regular paychecks from the bank for a long, long time. Some shit you just can't fake—back then an Agency employee could never have built that background. Obviously, that's why I was recruited in the first place. But now, for the first time, at one of the most important moments in the War on Drugs, and at probably the pinnacle of my success as an Agency operative, I am seriously, *woefully* regretting the day I said "I Do" and married-up with the Agency . . .

This G4 I'm on is one seductively sexy aircraft. It's got that long, sleek frame, like a long tall supermodel, her sleek wings swept way back and spread wide like she's opening up her bosom, two big, round, purring engines placed strategically down her torso for your optimum pleasure and powerful thrust as you ride her. Back in the day you got high just looking at her. Inside it's like Vegas—luxurious leather everywhere, from the rooflamers to the fully-reclining seats to the edges of the tabletops. Just about everything else was made of wood. Burled wood. Not the kind you find on a Mercedes dashboard, but the kind you find everywhere in a Rolls-Royce; and it's no coincidence that Rolls-Royce provides the engine power for this gorgeous Babe as well. Inside it can be set up in endless configurations, the huge swivel reclining rocking seats set up every which way but loose. And the sound, that soft, sweet, dull muffled roar that only a tamed, *sexy* beast will yield. And speaking of tamed sexy beasts, your host would normally provide in-flight entertainment as well. *Live.* So you might imagine how *jacked* some Colombian drug warriors would get in anticipation of that kind of ride. And yeah, back in the day, it was a thrill to get a chance to ride her, something you rarely, if ever, got the chance to do. But that day, for me, uh-uh. I wanted out so badly that I would have jumped if I could have gotten the door open.

I'm staring back at Chupacabra. *Trying not to shit my pants.* Not because this guy absolutely horrifies me, because he absolutely does, but because of what *I think I might have to do to him.* I am in so fucking far deep right now that there ain't no going back. *Ever!* Remember what I said about firefights? You can't just quit in the middle of one. Well, right now I am in the biggest goddamn firefight of my life, and it is raging at 40,000 feet, completely inside my pounding spinning skull-

"Fye *thou*-san, *Amigo!* He drops a perfectly crisp, sticker-wrapped pack of fifty $100 bills into the center of the pot. The other soldiers explode in a combination of screams, laughing jeering pounding the table like those fuckers in the Deerhunter and I'm like *Godfuckingfuckgodfuckingdammit!* I think I thought that about a thousand times in that millisecond. This sick, demented brother of el Diablo never liked me, never trusted me, always wanted to kill me and is now fucking taunting me! There's nobody left in this hand, and when he drops that cash on the pile, there's already twenty grand on the table. The others are taunting me as well, "Ay Maricon!" "Oooh Bendejo!" AYAYAY! They're all rolling around laughing, cheering, having a blast, in anticipation of who will win this titanic battle—the Gringo banker or the Chupacabra . . .

KILKENNY

I know he's got the full house. Jacks and 7's. He knows it. Everybody knows it. *They think I'm bluffing.* All I have is a pair of 4's showing. Nothing else, all black and red. No possible straight, no possible flush, *no possible shit*! They don't know what the Hell I have, but they know I'm bluffing. Now they want to see if I have the balls to see this thing through, this shit that I started, going after Chupacabra with this bluff. And win or lose, that cabin is going to erupt when I turn over my cards, so much so that *I hope the G4 rolls over in the air!* That might be the only thing that saves me.

Sadly, though, I'm not bluffing! But I'm not trying to win this hand either! The last three cards I was dealt, including the hole card, were 4's! I am holding four of a kind! That has never happened to me in a game I wasn't cheating at in my entire fucking life! Now, NOW I draw four of a kind? This is the cruelest of cruel jokes that God is playing on me! Payback for all the nasty shit I've done, I guess? But why me though, why not pay back that sick motherfucker across the table? I just can't believe this crap is happening . . .

Remember that "you're never so alive as when you're close to death" crap? Well, right now I'm not smelling any roses. I don't see any sunlight, I see only darkness. And the only thing I'm tasting is a little bit *of my own vomit*! I FEEL death, and *it's chilling-*

But it also sharpens my senses. There's no good way out of this. *God must play a part in the outcome.* If it was only about the money, that would be *easy*. I'd drop twenty grand, lose the bluff and just say "Fuck it." But I can't do that here. This may *look* like Vegas, but it ain't. I can't fold. Not because it would make me look weak, but because *the soldiers will pick up my cards.* They'll see all my lucky 4's. Their Orangutan brains will be flummoxed for a few seconds as to why I didn't lay them down. In any other place that might be enough time for me to get the Hell out, but not inside the Belly of this Sexy Beast, at 40,000 feet. They will soon realize that I quit because I was scared. Not scared of Chupacabra, but scared that I might piss him off by beating him. But at this point If I'm scared of that, then they'll be thinking I'm not who they think I am. Which probably means they'll think I'm DEA. *And then I become soup.*

But these guys are all about Machismo, Chupacabra being the embodiment. You don't fuck with that either. Humiliating Chupacabra, up here, in this game, in front of his crew, will result in my death as well. *He will not take it well.* His instinct will be to leap across the table and yank my throat out. He might succeed. *Remember, I've actually seen him do it!* I'm sure he will try. I'm not armed, of course, and the only things I can beat this guy at are IQ tests and Jeopardy! *And apparently now poker as well!* God must play the final hand in this fucked-up game he's orchestrated already. There's no other way-

I purposefully put the worried look on my face. The Colombians go quieter, whispering to each other while they think I'm contemplating quitting or not. I pick up my cards, peek, put them down. Then up again, peek. Then down. It's *deadly* quiet now. Not one whisper. They think I'm folding; I'm just hoping the cards will change every time I peek at them. *No such luck.* Ok, let's end this fucking thing-

"Aqui su *'fye* thou-san,' hijo de perra, y otra *TEN* THOU-SAN!!!!

KILKENNY

The G4 jerks sideways at the *explosion* from the soldiers. They are whoopingscreaminglaughing at Chupacabra "son of a bitch? He say 'you son of a bitch?!'" they can't be contained! A bunch of monkey savages beating the shit out of everything around them foaming at the mouth in anticipation while watching me slit my own throat. *Total fucking chaos.* Chupacabra jumps up ready to fucking kill but the game's not over! "Siente se Siente se" they start yelling at him—He sits back down. The soldiers go quiet again, whispering, mumbling. Chupacabra is drooling. *I think he has a hard-on as well.* I'm thinking now 'son of a bitch' wasn't the right move-

Ten grand. That's what it will cost Chupacabra to call my bluff. I know that's all he has left. *I counted.* There's now *fifty fucking thousand* on the leather-edged, burled-walnut custom poker table. And I'll take it from him, if I live.

Then suddenly, quietly . . .
"Tu mama esta chupando el pene del Diablo en el Infierno."

Yup, it was the wrong move—It's now finally turned for the worse. I can feel a sweat bead down the back of my neck. It's making my neck twitch, giving me a goosebump. In that culture you kill people over something like this. He just said that my mother is sucking the Devil's cock in Hell. *He sneered it at me.* The respect is gone. I know now, that I am dead. Gone. Warm soup. Unless I kill him first, of course, but that ain't looking so good . . . You just don't say that shit unless you plan on playing it out.

Jesus fucking Christ my wife just had our first kid, my son. I'm not ever going to see him again.

DOOMSDAY MARAUDERS

But I'm not laying down for this motherfucker either.

I immediately fire back:

"Donde se *ahogan* en la mia, tu MARICON!"
"Where you will choke on mine, you fucking FAGGOT!"

Nothing. He doesn't move. Nobody does. *They're all as white as the KLAN. They know this is blood. They're scared of me now, because obviously I'M OUT OF MY GODDAMNED MIND. Bluffing is one thing, but calling out the Chupacabra is a whole other thing they want no part of-*

"Show me Greeeengo." He speaks very, very slowly, drops the ten grand into the pile, and starts smiling. *Jesus he's got beautifully straight white teeth.* He knows he's won. He'll kill me later, take up the fifty grand and get laid twice a day for a month. This eases up the crowd again, some whispers now, a few laughs, but the tension is still high and tight-

"Ok dumbass-"

I drop the four of a kind on the pile and and there is stunning silence—It's taking a few seconds for it to sink into their little monkey-brains . . . shit, no, holy shit, oh My God He FUCKING WON!!! AYAYAYAYAY!!! they erupt at once jumping up and down yelling and screaming throwing each other around slapping me on the back saying *GENIUS GENIUS GENIUS the Banker GENIUS!!! Chupacabra Chupa Chupa Chupacabra he got fucked by the Banker oooooooohhhhhh el Diablo is gonna fuck him in the ass oooooooohhhhhhhh!!!* Now I'm like shh, *SSHH* guys shit c'mon I got lucky luck luck just fuckin' luck!!! *He fuck Chupa in the ass! He fuck Chupa in the ass!*

Maybe it was the fifty grand he lost, the warm temperature inside, the fact that I had the cojones to challenge him, all the screaming and taunting, or whether he really did fear El Diablo, but Chupacabra had turned a deep, bloody red. His eyes looked so contorted it looked like his head was in a vice. It took a minute or so to process all of this but when he did, HE JUMPED OVER THE GODDAMNED TABLE ON TOP OF ME STARTS BEATING MY FUCKING BRAINS OUT THEY'RE PULLING HIM HE NO MOVE JUST KEEPS HAMMERING MY SKULL THE LIGHTS ARE GOING OUT THEN-IT-**STOPS.**

Two of the soldiers have a chain pulled tight around his neck and two others have .45's laying along his temples. "El Jefe necesita este tipo, Chupa." *The boss needs this guy, Chupa.* In the end, the soldiers did their job. They're scared to death of Chupa, but the boss is the boss. They restore order to the pack. I get a reprieve, for now. *God played his hand.*

Fortunately, we were almost home. When we arrived Miami it's just after 10 o'clock, so I tell the whole crew and the pilots that we're going to "El Club," a private place that the boss controls. It's on me, all night, all comers, all everything. Liquor, coke, pot, and women. Lots and lots of women. It costs me about *fifty fucking thousand.*

Chupacabra didn't show. Just up and disappeared. He's Colombian though, not a U.S. citizen (we've always got eyes on him in the U.S.) so unless he's quitting the Cartel, which is suicide, he's gone home to Colombia somehow, to lick his wounds. That doesn't make me feel any better. He's more dangerous now than ever. He *will* kill me. He knows it. I know it. **Everybody knows it.** He'll find a reason, if I let him. But I won't. That next day I took a long vacation from the bank, and a leave of absence from the Agency. I never went back to Colombia again. I packed up my wife and newborn kid and moved to California. Using my real name, I transferred to a different part of the world. I give it all up, for now. But I'm alive.

A man's got to know his limitations . . .

So what do you think about that one? You believe me when I say that Pablo Escobar is still alive? He is, make no mistake-

What about me? You think I'm a pussy now because I packed it up and never went back to Colombia?

Pussy, no. Genius, yes. There's no way I remain alive if I set foot in Colombia again. Suicide is for, well, the suicidal! This I am not. And lest we forget the most important lesson from this, *A man's got to know his limitations.* As in our marauding operations, most of mine were psychological. In this case I pushed it as far as I could go. Remember my warnings about taking on SEALs or Marines straight-up? You just don't do it. Same thing here. I couldn't take out Chupacabra straight-up at anything, except maybe Scrabble or the SAT. It takes more brains and balls to know when you're beat, and to take something away from it. I took my life with me. Rolled-up the tent, hiked out, pitched it somewhere else. Chasing death is one thing, actually catching it is, well, crap! I almost did. So a few takeaways from this last little adventure that we need to apply to the prepper colony and as we move forward in general:

1. Always Keep Your Cool
2. Chase Death, Try Not To Catch It
3. Know Your Limitations
4. Sometimes You Just Have To Quit

In any case, I wasn't away from the business too, too long. Less than a year, and I wound up pitching my new tent over in West Africa. Hence all the crap in Liberia with Charles Taylor. Another fucking psychotic freak. And another story for another time—I had been working over there anyway for a couple of years, on and off while I was in Colombia. New country, same shit. Follow the money, take out the trash. I was getting too comfortable with that whole lifestyle down in Colombia anyway. New life, new wife, new kid, fresh start-

CHAPTER 10

Taking Down a Survivalist Colony

Ok so now we're playing in the big time. 50 people. A bunch of good shooters. Four or Five ex-military, maybe a SEAL or two. Well laid-out, well-fortified, easily defensible compound. You want it, you got it! As I described in the beginning of this book, I'm showing you how to do this in the form of fiction. Hopefully it will help you to form your own plans, get creative and be ready to figure it all out when the time comes. *Here we go-*

We spotted a long chain-link fence line from a couple of hundred feet below and a couple of miles away. Figured it might be a target of opportunity, so we started swinging down into the meadow and across, and came to the bottom of a steep hill, completely barren, maybe 30 degrees. It headed up for a few hundred feet, about a hundred vertical, then it angled sharply straight up to about 65 degrees for another hundred feet or so. The upper part of the hill is slate and scree, with some pretty soft deep dirt on the lower half. At the very top of the ridge is the chain link fence, running right along the edge for about 400'. No way we're getting up there from here. Somebody would have to be roped in and pulled up.

KILKENNY

If we want to see what's on the other side of that fence we're going to have to take the long way around, and I'm not sure how long that's going to be. We decide to set up for the night and head along the road around the bottom of the ridge in the morning.

5 miles. That's how far around the ridge we had to go before we could find a way up that wasn't more than 20 degrees. We make our way up the hills in the short rocky scrub and give the horses a breather. Now we have to head about 5 miles backwards to see if we can find what's hidden up here on the tabletop. It's certainly beautiful up here. Great views through the treeline, lots of evergreen mixed with maple. Not too thick a forest, and it looks like there's a long fire road or logging road headed right back through it in the direction we need to go. The hair on the back of my neck starts standing a little bit-

In the old days they would say *'this is ambush country.'* Though we haven't gotten any indication at all that are any other people around here, we're still about to head down a narrow dirt road bounded by trees on both sides, for about 5 miles to a destination that right now is only a chain link fence. Chain link fences, though, generally protect things on the inside and keep harmful things on the outside. From afar it looked strong and new, so my bet is there's something valuable there. And that means there might be someone looking out for it-

I'll say it again, when you're out and about conducting your operations in the next life, err on the side of caution. *We are not military. Nobody hands us an intelligence summary. There are no reinforcements. There is no evac. We cannot take casualties.*

So it's up to us to be careful and unconventional. We head about a quarter mile into the treeline, set up camp and picket the horses. We're waiting for nightfall.

It's a gorgeous Gibbon moon, plenty of light on such a clear night at this altitude. I mount up along with my sniper. The other two guys will stay at camp. They're gonna stuff all the sleeping bags, keep a good fire going in the center of our camp and then keep watch over it from outside the perimeter. If somebody's gonna come crawling up on us we want to know, and determine if they're there to take us out or not.

Sniper and I ride in the trees along the road for about 2 ½ miles before we dismount, tie up our horses, and head the rest of the way on foot, still in the trees. The dirt road skims along the edge of a gorgeously calm and black 20-acre lake. I'm betting it's loaded with smallmouth bass. *Have to try it sometime.* We get about two miles and the trees fall away . . . On our right is a tall cornfield, maybe three full acres. Up ahead further on the right and running along the road is a grove of trees, can't quite tell of what type from this distance. The dirt road dies out into a wide-open, flat and bare expanse of dirt for about three hundred yards, and at the end, shining like Christmas lights in the bright moonlight, is the galvanized chain link fence.

I pull out the Bushnell's and can see that it's about eight feet high, and running along the top are three lines of barbed wire, spaced about 6" apart, wrapped in concertina wire. Nice tight, big, looping spools, *well done*. This runs all along the length of the fence that we can see, and I'm looking out and down the line maybe 300 yards—On the left edge of the fence it starts to drop off down a steep hill again. About twenty feet in from that edge is the gate, and it's about ten feet wide. Typical chain link construction as well, with drop legs that slide into fixed steel-rimmed holes in the ground for added support. Reinforced along the top rail into the gate posts the same way. Again, very well done.

On the other side of the fence, set back about ten feet in that 20 foot section between the fence and the edge, sits a small guard tower, about 12 feet off the ground. Looks like aluminum construction, basically a glorified deer blind, but I'm betting the four-foot high walls are 3/8" steel reinforced. As I look again down the full length of the fenceline I can see what looks like two more. Somebody good put some real planning into this place. That means there's something in there worth protecting!

Can't see much else in this light without getting a lot closer, and we're not prepared for that so **WAIT** . . . there's movement . . . *Dogs!! Moving along the fenceline now, single file. A German Shepherd and a Dobie. Typical! Classic!* We decide to head on back to our mobile base camp to . . . **WAIT again** . . . *We're deadly still now. Even at 300+ yards we'll give them no reason to be alarmed. The Shepherd wants to keep moving, but the Dobie is hesitating—Well trained, I love those dogs! But he'll be the first one I take out anyway-*

As I was starting to say, we'll figure this all out in the morning.

So on the way back let's think about what we've discovered so far-

About five miles away down at the end of an old logging road is something protected by an 8' chain link fence with concertina topping, and a fortified entry gate. The fenceline has three guard towers every 300 feet or so, patrolled by dogs on the inner perimeter. The left edge drops off steeply down a ridge. *Good defensive posture.* There's a big lake nearby, *great water supply.* At least three acres of corn. *Renewable food supply.* A big wide-open space between all that and the fence, *the Dead Zone.* Well-designed, well constructed, *Expensive.* This is a community, for sure, with lots of food, supplies and I'm betting, weapons as well. From the little we saw it was professionally designed from a security perspective, especially the location, with steep drops on at least two sides limiting the areas you really need to defend. Probably there's a few ex-military on site as well. We'll head out again tomorrow in the daylight to try and see what's really going on in there-

Dawn breaks beautifully down here in deep southwestern Colorado, especially up in the hills around Durango at about 3000 feet. It's gonna be a beautifully warm day, the sun is rising fast and the heat's already picking up. I let Sniper sleep in a little bit longer and take one of the other guys back out with me. We'll all meet up back at our permanent base camp about 25 miles from here sometime tomorrow. We're gonna need more food, bullets and equipment to get what we want from this place if my thinking's correct. Besides, I don't want to be laying around here at night once we let them know what we're up to. If there's military on the other side of that fence I don't want them hunting us—just yet. We'll go take a daytime peek then rendezvous and develop our plan.

Okay. I'm now officially intrigued. We've obviously stumbled onto a very sophisticated, very intelligent, well-designed community, and it must have cost those living there now *huge dollars* in the old life to buy into this thing, or be a part of it as it was being put together. Which by extrapolation tells me that they have *warehouses* full of stuff, including guns and ammo and medical supplies. Clearly they have dogs, maybe there are horses? Maybe women? *This is the mother lode!* The only problem is, how do we take from it what we want without getting killed? If I had the chance I'd also like to chat with these guys to see what's in their heads. Usually we come up against morons or those retarded Doomsday Preppers. This gang is different . . . Where are they going with all of this . . . Are they just trying to get by until society possibly re-forms (not happening), are they just living out their days, or are they going to attempt to find other colonies and re-establish civilized society? Is this a monarchy, oligarchy, democracy, theocracy? I have great respect for other Intel and ex-military of course, so I'd love to chat with them as well. Unfortunately, that's probably not going to happen . . . and if it does it probably won't be a wide-ranging, thought-provoking, intellectual conversation . . . probably something more like "OK who dies first?"

. . . As we approach that big, dark beautiful lake we stop, dismount and start walking the horses carefully, slowly, heading south around that east edge that hugs the logging road. We stay inside the treeline, and keep a really sharp eye cast out over the road and the lake beyond. Stepping quietly now we are passing just beyond it, and I turn and glance back at this gorgeous piece of mountain majesty. *God Fucking Dammit.* Nestled up in a big wide Douglas Fir, on the north edge of the lake right on the edge of the logging road and looking out over *everything,* is a deer stand. Only it's about 40 feet up the tree. *Crap!* There's nobody in it, but now the game's changed. *These guys are serious.* I'm impressed. And a little more nervous as well. Let's see what lies ahead before I jump to my new conclusion-

Sure enough, about a quarter mile past the lake and down the logging road, there it is—a tripwire, slung long and low across the logging road. I'm not ready yet to see what it's hooked to, if anything, so we skirt far and wide into the trees. I'm sure it was there last night, but we weren't riding in the most logical route to actually "trip" it. As we get within a few yards of the Dead Zone we locate another trip wire, this one slung low across the logging road as well and two more deer stands, opposing each other across the logging road, about 50 yards apart and 40 feet up. *Nice little kill zone they've set up here-*

Okay I'm sold. We're not dealing with regular military here, or even Marines or SEALs. This has Green Beret written all over it. *Fucking Whack-a-Moles!* This has now become a very dangerous place. Maybe nobody has paid these guys a visit in a long while, maybe never, but next time they leave the compound these guys will find our tracks for sure, as they will do a thorough sweep outside the Dead Zone and up on towards the lake. That's just part of what they do.

So what now?

Obviously this changes the whole Goddamned thing. This is where I might usually say "Do we really need anything these guys may have that's worth taking on at least one Green Beret?" Not to mention, too, the guard towers and dogs as well? Usually the answer is Hell No! But as I've already agreed to take you folks on this little ride, and because this is probably the best haul we will ever find, then Hell Yes! Let's do it!

In which case it means no fun and games, no avoiding collateral damage, people are probably gonna get hurt, it is what it is, etc. etc. So Katie bar the door and let's start the ball!

For some reason today I grabbed the M4. Maybe it was that tingly feeling I've had since I've been around here. The .30-30 was already in the scabbard. We're not wearing armor, though, as this was supposed to be a long-range visual recon mission. Obviously we discovered more than we wanted to, and you can bet the house that they've got more tricks up their sleeves. The thing about Green Berets, in my experience, is that you're better off taking them on if you know where they are. That's obvious. They don't like to be holed-up, they'd rather be out and about and hitting you by surprise from up, below and sideways. So the best thing to do if you're gonna take these guys on is to keep them boxed-in. Contained. Don't let them get out. They get anxious and try to get out, and they're pretty damn good at it, but sometimes they make mistakes when they get restless. *Sometimes.*

So my dilemma right now is this: If we pack it up now and go meet up with the rest of our gang tomorrow to develop a plan, there's a good chance that by the time we get back here to implement it those guys on the other side of the fence will have discovered evidence of our little visits. That will eliminate our 'surprise' advantage, put them on high alert, force them to start laying more traps for us, and probably put at least one of them outside the fence. If we stay, however, it's just two of us against *howevermanyof* them, with very little food or ammo. And our other guys won't know what we're doing. Any suggestions?

Just kidding. My buddy and I are gonna stay right where we are for now, and come up with our new plan. Then he's gonna ride back and catch up with the others, raid the storage lockers and come on back (riding fresh horses). I'm gonna stay here, under cover, and keep an eye on the place. I figure if we get the plan together in a couple of hours, the whole gang can be back around 2am. *Perfect!*

Tom takes my horse back with him. We're hoping that if these guys do come out today and find all the tracks we're leaving, they'll see that two riders came and left today, and that's it— And not realize I'm still here. *Hopefully.* I spend the rest of the day keeping a sharp eye out for any movement around the compound . . .

Well, there's a lot of it! I can hear voices talking, friendly tones, a little laughing here and there, no indication of any urgency, stress or fear, as there might be if they knew we were watching. I couldn't see anybody, even with the glass, but they were out and around their colony doing whatever it is they do. I even had time to scout around the edge of the Dead Zone, looking for more wires, traps, anything out of place. Nothing new. I searched around the bases of the trees holding the deer stands, no traps over there either. Climbed both of them, as the U-shaped metal spikes drilled in as stairs were on the sides of the trees away from the compound. *Their first mistake!* No booby traps waiting in the stands. I did notice, however, that there were spotlights affixed to the tops of the guard towers. *Reminds me of a fucking Nazi concentration camp. I hate Nazis.* This is good though, because if I'm as smart as I think I am, it will help our plan!

Nobody left the compound during the day. Right before sunset, though, the big gate lumbered open and a modified (read extended) jeep wrangler came rolling out, filled with big wooden barrels. At this distance they look like wine barrels. A driver and a passenger, riding shotgun. Literally. Looked like he was holding my CZ Coachgun! They drove in a straight line from the gate through the Dead Zone toward the logging road. Right before it they veered left in between two pines, doing a little jog around the tripwire. *Well it's definitely live, probably the others as well.* I'm assuming they were heading out to the lake, but I wasn't about to break cover and go check. They came rolling on back about an hour later, a little slower, a little lower. Obviously they had watered up at the lake. At the end of the road they did the little jog again, then straight through the Dead Zone. The big gate lumbered shut behind them, and just as the sun set, the dogs were out on patrol. Only this time I think there were three. I say "think" because the Shepherd looked leaner and darker the second time I saw him. *Glad they're guard dogs and not coonhounds! They'd have sniffed my ass even at this distance-*

I packed it on up right then and headed over to the lake myself to rendezvous with the rest of the gang. Once the sun set it got dark pretty fast, so I didn't think there was any chance at that point of any other 'outside the fence' activity from the compound. I was getting a little edgy anyway-

The boys showed up around midnight. A little bit early as they apparently had an easy go of it. After that long ride they can take about an hour's nap, which is all they'll need, so things are working out perfectly. I'm gonna snooze as well; we've got four dogs to keep watch for us. They brought the two border collies and two of our own German Shepherds. Remember when I talked about how the Border Collies find out what's going on, then come let us know? Well, this is where it comes in handy. No worries about getting whacked while we sleep. These smart, stealthy, toothy beasts will handle the watch. We discuss the plan, go into detail regarding tonight's activities, then crash at about 1am. We've got a big, *big* middle of the night ahead.

We rouse at about 2am, and the dogs start getting excited. They know the drill. We don't wake up like this on the trail unless we're gonna go have some fun! Hopefully we won't lose any of them this time around. There's a good chance though-

Ok one more time we go over the plan and timing for tonight. We're taking one of the border collies and one shepherd with us, the others will stay at our camp. We leave the horses behind and head out in the trees along the logging road, in the gorgeously soft bright moonlight. I almost need sunglasses. A beautiful night for hunting!

KILKENNY

First Move, Psychological Warfare

We're staring out across the Dead Zone. We've been timing the dogs' little circuit trail around the compound and along the fence that fronts it, and although not quite regular, it seems like they show up at one end or the other about every 15-20 minutes or so. There's very little breeze tonight but it's a soft downwind anyway, so they're not sniffing us or stopping.

The boys brought back all of the empty bottles of beer and Jack Daniels that we had, and we filled about a hundred of them at the lake, then cork-stopped them. We used up just about all of the piano wire we had tying them together, about every ten feet. That's about a one-thousand foot line, a hell of a lot of work, but a *very* important piece of the plan.

We give the dogs about two minutes after making their long pass inside the fence along the Dead Zone. *Move Out!* We slink up to within about a hundred feet of the fence, and quietly, carefully, start laying out the long line of wire and bottles, standing them up straight, along the entire front of the fence line. We need to get this done in about 10 minutes. *No time for dawdling!* About halfway across we leave a big sign, bent over into a triangle so it stands in plain view, stating our demands:

- 10,000 rounds of ammo
- one of those wine barrels
- six months of food for 8 (they don't know we're only four)
- 6 months of fuel
- The Jeep (I know, I know, they won't like that)

We get the last bottle up, and drag the remaining piano wire back into the trees. No sooner than we get there and the dogs are at the far end of the fence. We stop, drop and quit breathing. The Dobie, again, knows something's up, sees the string of bottles, probably smells a trace of us. He starts whining a bit, but the shepherd isn't buying it, and again, tries to keep the two going. Uh-uh, *The Dobie will have none of it!* He's staying. *Goddamn smart dog I was counting on him!* He starts barking, and that's our *GO* signal! We pull on the tripwire crossing the logging road at the edge of the Dead Zone from about a hundred feet away and BOOBOOBOOM!!! Three grenades detonate, leaving a nasty trench crossing the logging road. *Glad we didn't stumble over that!* By now the lights are coming on and a siren goes off *just like in a fucking concentration camp!* We left sniper back at the other tripwire and we hear the same BOOBOOBOOOM! from up his way. The three of us then spread out across the trees and into the cornfield on the right, M4-s ready. After a few minutes we can hear a little barking of orders, some muffled shouting, running around inside the compound and soon the towers are manned and the spotlights flash on. We give them about 60 seconds to lock in on the string of bottles and piano wire strung along the fence line, a hundred feet out. *They do.* We give them another 60 seconds to process this, then each of us lets loose one shot each CRACRACRACK with our M4's, putting out each of the three spotlights. We think this should keep them inside the compound for now—our work is now done for the evening . . .

Well, you might imagine what's going on inside the compound right about now—a little bit of confusion, a little bit of fear, and the foreboding realization that there actually are bad guys out there. Preparing for this is one thing, but actually having to deal with it is quite another. Hell I'll bet it was probably "fun" and "exciting" in their old life thinking and planning on surviving a fall of society. Well, now it's upon them. And there's nothing like the smells and sounds of war to steel your insides, *or make you pee your pants—*

I'll bet there's a lot of peeing going on right now. The regular folks in there are now realizing that *people might actually get hurt, or ohmygod even die!* There might even be a little trepidation among any ex-military in there. Not the Green Berets, though. There may be only one or two in there, but that's enough. They're probably happy that this finally happened; they were probably bored to death! And it's those guys that are now taking account of the situation:

- An unknown group of raiders has set off explosives tied to two of the colony's tripwires.
- When the spotlights came on, they were allowed to stay on for approximately 2 minutes, long enough to assess the exterior situation, then were expertly shot out.
- There is a long string of what looks like Improvised Explosive Devices running parallel to the front fenceline, approximately 100 feet off.
- They have put in writing that they want food, ammo, a water container and the Jeep.
- These guys are clearly Pros.

Well, what should they do? Obviously this appears to be a frontal attack, which makes sense as there's on old logging road, a wide-open field and a big water supply in that direction. And also given the fact that the back of the colony fenceline sits along the edge of a really steep ridge, and that nobody would survive coming at them that way. All true. But just as much as we can only get at them one way, they can only get out one way as well. *If we're vigilant!*

It's dead quiet for about two hours. As we suspected, though at least one of these guys shows balls. He climbs up the back fence with a rope attached to him, and starts up over the top. We know this because as soon as his boots hit the dirt they get all dusted-up from Sniper's M4. We can hear it loud and fast. He puts about 20 rounds into the dirt below and around the guy's feet and he leaps back over the fence like a high jumper! We anticipated this, of course, as after Sniper set off the tripwire up the road earlier, he hightailed it around to the back of the fence line, down the ridge a ways. Sat fully protected in trees and boulders waiting for this to happen.

Now we've got 'em bottled up. Even the Green Berets understand the situation. Mike climbs the tree stand overlooking the Dead Zone, and launches one of our arrows into the compound. It has a very simple note wrapped around it:

"Have the Jeep at the edge of the road where it meets the cornfield at noon. The driver stays. We will turn him loose when we feel the Jeep, ammo and food are not rigged. If they are rigged, the driver doesn't come back. Nobody has to die now. Play it smart and we promise, you won't see us again for another year."

We've given them until noon, and given that it's just about sunrise, that doesn't leave them too much time to decide what to do-

These guys are between a rock and a hard place—honestly, I don't know what I'd do if I—*NO NO NO that's bullshit*. I'd come right at me, full bore, call my bluff. Try to make me take casualties, and waste ammo. I wouldn't act like I had all that food and ammo by just giving it to me, that would be stupid. Now, given that I'm really a nice guy and that *I would* actually leave, with me that's the smart play. For anyone else, stupid. But of course they don't know that.

Well, these guys aren't stupid. At least they're not acting that way, just yet. Noon comes and goes, nothing. I probably would have been disappointed, a little, had they just rolled-over. I know there's a Green Beret or two in there just itching to take me out, so I wouldn't want them to just lay down. That's un-American! But they didn't disappoint.

Second Move, Intimidation!

Now it's our turn, of course, so we go relieve Sniper and take turns napping. We're not leaving, just waiting for nightfall. They know it too. Remember, there's plenty of regular folks in there, little kids, old people. Most of them are frazzled, exhausted, scared, nervous, on edge. That makes them fractious, and as I've said before, prone to mistakes and misjudgment.

We, on the other hand, are completely relaxed, hydrating, eating, resting up for tonight. It may turn out to be another long one.

DOOMSDAY MARAUDERS

You remember now that the boys raided our storage lockers before they came back, so we're fully-loaded with all kinds of goodies. As these nice folks were polite enough to refuse our offer, *without so much as a 'No Thank You' card*, well, we're going to let them know now that we're here until we get what we want, or we get our asses kicked, or some of them die. It's ultimately going to be their call. We've picked this fight, for sure, but they'll have the opportunity to end it, if they want. So here we go—

We've got the back side covered by Sniper again. *He loves that shit!* I gave him the opportunity to pick the time he would like to kick this thing off. Sniper, by nature, is a very patient type, having lived about four of his eight years in the Corps lying prone undercover in the weeds. Needless to say *I am much less patient*, and by the time we had a full moonrise I'm practically jumping up and down ready to go. I would have started half an hour earlier! But Sniper is Sniper for a reason, and I'm sure he's got one, so I'll just keep biting down hard on a little piece of rope until CRAACK . . . There he goes . . . CRAACK . . . Quiet again . . . CRAACK . . . We obviously don't know what he's doing, but 3 means *GO!* anyway so we're off and running— First thing we do is get about 20 yards deep into the cornfield, spray out as much kerosene as we can across a row parallel to the compound fence, and let a few Cocktails fly—smash, crackle, smash crackle, smash crackle, you know the drill, then WHOOOOSH WHOOOOSH WHOOOOSH! And the cornfield is starting up in flames. That little downwind breeze from last night is gone, so the flames will find their way toward the easiest air, and that's up and over and towards the wide-open Dead Zone, in full view of the colonists.

There are FOUR dogs now at the fenceline, barking almost rabidly—Three Shepherds and that really smart Dobie. Remember I said I'd take him out first? Well, I changed my mind. *I like that goddamned dog! I'm gonna take him as a souvenir!* So the boys, of course, are quite surprised as I pull out the M4, pin the laser tail on the donkey and squeeze off a shot that makes the Shepherd closest to the gate go down. *Crappy shot!* I think I just hind-quartered him, so I squeeze off another and *Thwack*! Put him out of his pain. The boys are looking at me like, 'What the fuck? Quit wasting ammo!' Mike then one-shot's the head off a second Shepherd at the far end of the fenceline. That leaves one Shepherd and one Dobie (mine) that we can see. Sniper of course hears the 3 shots, of course, then unloads along the back fenceline. I have no idea what the hell he's doing, but he's *clearly* up to no good. All of a sudden I see a little bit of flame all the way into the back of the compound. I can smell the smoke too. His M4 barrage stops. I fire 3, then he fires 3. *We're sending somebody over*—Mike's headed over to spend the night with Sniper, just in case those sneaky sons of bitches try to get out the back again. They'll take turns sleeping tonight, and Mike's got some Slim Jims and a six-pack of Coke with him. We'll save the beer and Jack for when this is over-

We know that the colonists know that we're signaling each other, it's pretty simple after all, but I didn't want to use the radios, as those smart-ass green berets in there might be listening for us. Not taking any unnecessary chances with this bunch-

DOOMSDAY MARAUDERS

Ok so we're done for the night, Tommy takes first watch over the front of the compound while I head back to our campsite to re-supply and check on the dogs. On the way there and back (uneventful), let's review the situation, again, from the colonists' perspective. First, from last night:

- An unknown group of raiders has set off explosives tied to two of the colony's tripwires.
- When the spotlights came on, they were allowed to stay on for approximately 2 minutes, long enough to assess the exterior situation, then were expertly shot out.
- There is a long string of what looks like Improvised Explosive Devices running parallel to the front fenceline, approximately 100 feet off.
- They have put in writing that they want food, ammo, a water container and the Jeep.
- These guys are clearly Pros.

Then this morning around dawn:

- An arrow comes zinging into the compound in the middle of the big recreation yard, sticking up and out like a javelin at the Olympics
- It has a note attached to it telling us to have the stuff they want out at the edge of the cornfield where it meets the road by noon.
- The driver stays with the raiders until they're sure none of the stuff we give them is booby-trapped.
- If anything is booby-trapped, they will kill the driver.
- They say if we comply, they will leave, but return next year.
- We don't comply.

Then after tonight's events;

- The colony is hit first from the backside down the hill from a sniper
- The raiders out front set our cornfield on fire
- They shot and killed two of our German Shepherds
- The barn out back caught fire from the barrage up the back hill from their sniper. Ignited an outside propane tank next to a plastic gas can left there by mistake. It took most of us to contain it.
- They have stopped shooting at us, and nothing seems to be happening.

Ok, so that's a lot of shit happening in 24 hours! So let's imagine, again, what the State of Nature in the compound is really like right about now-

Panic. Consternation. Exhaustion. Fear. Divided loyalties. Non-consensus. Crying. Arguments. Fraction. *Perfect!*

Really, just think about it, there's 18 men and 18 women of various ages, 14 children. All the children are horrified. The cornfield is burning, and two of the colony's dogs, maybe ones they played with, have been shot dead. Their barn caught fire as a result of our sniper. The women, as well, are terrified. For themselves, and their kids, especially. *They know now, this is war.* They weren't expecting this. Never in their wildest dreams. All of the colonists in there thought that there might be raiders, sooner or later, but nothing like this, *nothing like us!* The arguments have begun-

"Give them what they want, it's not that much!"
"If we give in now they'll want more!"
"Don't believe them they're testing our fortitude!"
"Give it up, we have nothing to lose right now!"
"We can't give up the Jeep!"

As I said before, *I would come right at me*. But that's just me. In any other situation, under siege, if you have plenty of whatever it is they want, give it up. They'll either go away, or not. If you don't give it up, they're probably not going away without drawing a little blood. So for these nice people, the right move, after having their cornfield burn, two good dogs shot dead and a barn explosion, is to give it up. If they have plenty, and we think they do, it's no sweat for them. If we don't go away, well, then the fight is forced on them-

So really, it looks pretty bad for them. No good choice. But it also has me worried a little bit. *Why?* Because there wasn't any real resistance. No laydown, no suppression fire, no directed shots out of the compound—Again, *Why?* Well, maybe they're actually not that good—*Nah!* Maybe they were worried about the kids in there, they weren't locked down right, our timing hit them badly, again, *Nah!* So what could it possibly be? Well, after everything that's gone on so far, I'm pretty sure it's been a *Threat Assessment*. Again, I'm officially impressed. Some of them in there are Pros as well. They were measuring us, I think, testing us, just as we were testing them. *Awesome!* **Finally a goddamn worthy adversary! We're gonna' have trouble when we show up again-**

KILKENNY

Third Move, Attack Prep!

Ok folks well I'm sure you all know what time it is again, *Recon!* A lot has gone on, obviously, so now we have to re-assess ourselves, especially given the fact that I think we have been measured as well. It's not gonna' be too hard, as we haven't really left this place like we usually do, to drive up the level of fear and exhaustion in the other side. My only worry now, though, is that one of those fucking whack-a-moles got loose. The guy up over the back fence might have been a diversion... Maybe while we were focused on taking out the dogs ... Or maybe while we were switching out positions ... These are what I refer to as *Choke Points*, those little parts of any mission plan that are the weakest, and usually the quickest. They last only a second or two, but for the highly skilled, that's enough. I'll give you an example: when a carjacking attempt on the streets of Detroit is taking place, the point at which the car driver and the car jacker *switch places* is the choke point. If there's a weakness in the plan, it's right there. As you pass each other, if you have the balls, that's when you make your move.

Although my guys are well-hidden, I'm a little nervous—*Time to use blue!* I'm changing up the plan on the fly now. I need to stay covered on the way back. I'm taking the headgear, *and I'm bringing the dogs too!*

I know we're gonna lose one, maybe both. *The colony knows* that the only shot they have at this is to get somebody outside the fence. I'm more sure than ever now that they have. That little hair on the back of my neck is standing up again. Sometimes you just know it. We're in the danger zone now, no bullshit.

And neither Ice nor Maverick is our wingman. If he really is a Green Beret, and I'm pretty goddamn sure, then he's gonna' do some damage before he's done. We've got a real fight on our hands. *Time to muscle-up!*

I start tossing the ball about a quarter mile out from the Dead Zone, buried deep in the trees off the logging road. The Shepherd and Collie are trampling about, far and wide-ranging, in their searches and retrievals of that little round, neon green piece of wonderment. Why are dogs so fixated on balls? Especially tennis balls? *Really!* In this case though, thank God. Two things are happening now: pretty soon Sniper and Mike (or Tommy) will hear the dogs, and know I'm hunting. Mr. Green Beret will figure it out sooner or later as well. This puts us on a deadly collision course. The dogs will eventually find him, or he'll try to take one out. Either way, we've got him. Hopefully not *them*. What happens then is up to him. If he gives it up, he might live. The risk to us, of course, is that if he's hands up, and we start talking, somebody else out there or in the compound might try to nail us. That wouldn't be their wisest choice, though, as Mr. Hands Up will die as well. I think they're smarter than that. *I think they just didn't figure on our little doggies.*

Well Hell, we're gonna' know soon enough. I'm sure my boys know what's up by now, but no sign of the Enemy. I'm gonna' give the dogs a rest after this last toss and BOOMPH! *Fuc . . . What's happnnniiingg, iiiii"m'mm"m ooooh I""mmm on oonnn my aasss cccaaaantt bbbreeeeeethhhhe wwhhatt thhe* fuck GodDAMNNIT I JUST TOOK A SLUG TO THE CHEST FROM THATFUCKINGWHACKAMOLE now I'm down. My hearing is gone, my eyes are cloudy, and I still can't breathe, but it's all coming back. *Slowly.* To hit me that hard damn fucking dead on the breast bone with that blunt force it must've been a .45. from not too far away. And I didn't see it, or him. *Dammit! Asshole! I hate getting shot. For all I know my breastbone is cracked. Sure fucking feels that way! Every breath is Hell. These motherfuckers are gonna' bleed now.*

I can start to hear now the suppression fire, from the colony. AR-15's. Really goddamn loud, three shooters. They're laying down the route for their boy to get back home. *Son of a fucking bitch! He got the drop on me!* Pat myself on the back, though, for donning the Level IIIa back on the trail. Again, man, *straight up these guys are Death!* I'm just a little more savvy, a little luckier, that's all-

It stops and Sniper and Tommy start giving it back, from the cover of the tall pines. *They're too close together.* I hobble on over as they're laying it down. On the way through the trees I see the Border Collie is down. Dead. The Shepherd too. Time to change the plan. *Again!*

Now, something you all need to know about me if you haven't figured it out already; I can be a little hot-headed. My biggest weakness, of course, and something I've attempted to tame over the course of my lifetime. Sometimes with success, sometimes without. I never know when my cooler head will prevail. Right now though, the cooler head is losing. I just got bushwhacked by a Green Beret, have a busted breastbone, lost my Shepherd and my Border Collie and got fucking outfoxed. *That pisses me off!* Apparently I cracked my head on the way down to the ground too, as it is now *throbbing*, there's a huge-ass knob on the back of it and I feel like vomiting. *A fucking concussion! Great! I love fighting when I'm completely fucked-up! This is great! Don't you just love it! Who's fucking idea was this any way!! Goddamn cocksucking motherfuc-*

"Kilkenny."

"What!"

"Kilkenny."

"*What!* What the fuck . . ."

"Muscle—up man. We gotta' make these assholes pay."

Well, there it is folks. That's why this is a team operation. A family, really. Just a few words from Sniper, delivered as quietly and calmly and slowly as a parent reading out loud to a small child, is all it took for me to get my grip back. *God Bless these guys!* Ok now I've got the steely-eyes going. I'm pissed, but under control. We all knew that sooner or later we'd lose a dog, maybe two. That Border Collie, though, was a *crewmember*. He'll be missed. We'll mourn him after. For damn sure now I'm taking their Dobie.

"Ok Sniper, thanks. In my pack I've got some sourdough, jerky and coke. Take a bunch, a couple thousand rounds and three tear gas cans too. Then you and Mike head back around the bottom. Me and Tommy are gonna' hang out here til' it gets dark. We're gonna keep these motherfuckers so bottled in they're gonna want to kill themselves . . ."

I am so deadly calm now that it even makes the boys nervous. They've seen this movie before. It doesn't end without blood. And right now I don't care whose it is, as long as it comes pouring out from under that galvanized chain link fence. I explain the rest of the revised plan, we all agree, with a few little tweaks. Sniper and Mike load up and head out. I will start the final push tonight. No *"Third Move, Attack Prep" on this day. They've forced us straight into attack.*

If this were a colony without any strong evidence of ex-Special Ops guys, or if we knew there was only one, I would have packed the gang up, headed back to our home base for a few days, rested up, and let the colony sit on their ass in anticipation of our return. I can't do that here. If we don't finish this now I'm sure they'll get another guy outside the fence, maybe next time he takes a head shot. We can't leave. Gotta bottle 'em up right here and now, then close in and end it-

We got the sourdough from that beautiful little ranch that we finished off on our last raid, so it really was quite the treat. Especially when you combine it with cold, pre-cooked mini-hot dogs out of the can. Just slather on a few mustard packs and *Damn,* it almost tastes like life before the Fall! So Tommy and I chill a little, eating those delicious sandwiches and drinking Coke. Not so bad! A couple of shots of Jack Daniels would have made this completely complete, but, well, we'll save that for our little victory party. I'm sure we're gonna have one now. We're all in . . .

Hopefully you can see where I'm taking all of this. I usually try to avoid killing people straight-up for no good reason. Usually leaves a bad taste in my mouth. Especially when it's basically good people, or ex-military. I wish they hadn't shot me in the chest. They've gone all-in, so now we have to as well, or lose, and worse maybe get killed as well. Remember what I said earlier in this book about getting into a firefight? This will all be over by sun-up. Either we'll be dead or they've rolled over. There's no other possible outcome at this point, as the plan has us pulling out all the stops, with no worries about collateral damage. In fact I'm expecting it. We need to leave a little blood on the floor. Sorry if that offends you. *Tough Shit! Muscle-up!*

It's a long, gorgeous evening, with a really long beautiful sunset. I don't think there's any prettier place in this country, pre-Fall or post-Fall. A warm, slow breeze, no mosquitos buzzing. Quiet now, with a few toads and crickets just starting to chirp. *A good day to die.* Not for us, of course, but for them–

About two hours later it's full-on night, with just about a full moon. Good news that the sky and sunset were so brilliant; bad news is that there are few clouds to cover up that gorgeous moon. We lose a little bit of advantage, but not enough to change anything. Night is night, and sometimes the bright moonlight can play tricks on your night vision goggles or scopes or lasers. If they've got them (I'm sure they do), it will hurt them more than it will us. We're running this thing tonight, they'll be playing defense. That's always harder–

We get one more snooze in, then rouse about a couple of hours before dawn. *Let's kick this thing off!* I start laying down a heavy suppression fire into and along the front fenceline, down and back along its entire length, as fast as I can keep reloading the M4. Tommy, now positioned on the other side of what's left of the cornfield, starts doing the same thing, except he's shooting about 20 feet up into the trees over the compound, just in case they've decided on an elevated position and also to start clipping a bunch of branches. He succeeds at both, as we hear a guy bark as he gets clipped and a bunch of debris is now raining down from the trees on top of the colony. As soon as my first shots went off Sniper opened up on them from the back side and below, leaving a little alley way for Mike to hustle-up through.

I'm sure the colonists are *not* loving this. They think they've killed one of us, which usually means one of two things: the side that lost a guy leaves and licks it wounds, or it gets really pissed. I'm sure that because we lost a guy (in their minds), we had a close call, they outfoxed us, etc., they were hoping that we would pack up and lick our wounds. *Nope!* Now they're dealing with the realization that this is for keeps. That recognition, if you've never experienced a fight to the finish, can be very, very emotionally crippling. And scary as well! This is when people start to panic, become unsure, get ready to pack it in. I'm sure a bunch of the men are not there yet, but I bet all of the women, older folks and kids all are. That means you can't count on them. *They're now a liability.* I talked about this earlier in the book as well. You have to be able to rely on your family members to shoot someone when you tell them too, otherwise you might as well *shoot them!* as they will be no good to you-

I can hear that the shooting has stopped from the other side of the colony, so we know that Mike is in position. We stop shooting in front as well. We're gonna take a few minutes to reload all of our magazines, and get ready for round two. I know it seems like a tremendous waste of ammunition, but these guys are for real, we think that we'll get it all back and well *do you have a better plan??*

We're also taking a break because we want the psychological factor to take a good, strong hold. They're under a smothering siege right now, and we've only just begun. The anticipation of what happens next must be killing them. *The Whack-a-Moles are stuck in their cages.* We launch another arrow with a message attached into the center of the colony. Easy to place it now as the tree cover up top has been quite a bit chewed away. It says:

"Thanks for making our lives a little more entertaining, as we've been getting pretty bored lately. You having fun right now? We hope so. Anyway, if you want to end the festivities, just let us know. You can do that by hanging a towel over the fence, or by starting a fire in plain view. Then at sun-up you can deliver the goods and we'll be on our way. Or not, and we keep playing. And as we're now down a couple of dogs, we also now politely request that you surrender that beautiful Doberman too. Oh, and because we've had so much fun, we now need 50,000 rounds of ammo, preferably AR-15, as well. Thanks!"

Actually, we're just kidding about letting them surrender just yet, even if they want to. We are not going to take any chances, and we are going to pound this lesson home. We can see that they've retrieved the arrow, we give them about 15 minutes to talk about it and then without any warning at all *Craaack CraaackCraaackCraaackCraaackCraaackCraaackCraaackCraaak*

I unload and the whole goddamned thing starts all over again. This time everyone of us is shooting directly into the compound, as we've cleared the overhead and Mike is hanging around the fenceline in back, fully-armored, under cover, and firing into the colony as well. Even if they had reached consensus to give it up they don't have the opportunity right now. They're holing-up again as the heavy storm of lead and clouds of acrid smoke fill the air around them and burns up their insides.

We can hear the women and kids screaming now, some guys yelling, others barking orders. No use. They can't do a goddamned thing until we let up again. *Except that we don't. We're stepping up the psychological pressure.* Mike lets loose a pretty damn good spread of the three separate tear gas containers. This clearly is a special occasion for us, as we've been saving some of our stash for just this kind of attack. *Yay!* Tear gas scares the shit out of everybody.

Tommy and I hold up in the front while Mike and Sniper keep hammering away in the back—What we're accomplishing here, successfully of course, is pushing the colonists away from the back of the complex, toward the center and closer to the front fenceline. Classic squeeze. They can't tough it out in the gas, and they don't want to get sliced and diced by the fenceline. We stopped shooting in front to give them the chance to get a little closer, and they have. Screaming, crying, shouting all the way. As more and more of them flee the hail of bullets and the cloud in back, Tommy and I open up again in front, this time shooting in the air a few feet over their heads.

In this gorgeous pre-dawn moonlight we can see them there, huddled down flat on the ground covering their heads, praying. I'm sure that this will come to an end soon. And it does. Tommy and I pull up, then Sniper puts a hold on it as well. Mike tosses another can over the back fence for good measure. After a couple of minutes of dead calm, we see a small, wiggly bright orange outline, getting larger, more yellow, and pretty soon it's a full-on bonfire. At the same time we notice two of the colonists approaching the fenceline. They toss a bright white sheet over it. Guess they want to make sure we got the message. *Just like we made damn sure they got ours.*

I grab the Walther and with a slow little POP . . . POP . . . POP send a message to Sniper to stay alert but stand down. We also assume that the colony will accept this rather small caliber triple shot as a sign of our acknowledgement that they've given it up. It's getting pretty close to sun-up right about now, so I expect they're gathering the supplies we need, and figuring out who is going to drive them out to us. I'm sure it will be the guy who shot me. He's got the stones. And the skills.

Just as the sun starts peaking over the eastern part of this high valley, I pull out my CZ-75B and fire off two slow shots. Sniper knows the sound of the CZ and that means come on up and join us. *Carefully!* The colonists, having at least half a brain, should also take this as a sign that we want them to get things rolling. They actually do, and fire two slow shots of somethingorother back. *How cute!*

Maybe 20 minutes or so later Sniper and Mike arrive at our position in the treeline just about the time that the colony's front gate starts lumbering sideways. They snuck along the outside fence on the steep side, knowing the game was up, and having tear gas and M4's ready, just in case.

About a minute later we see the Jeep, all weighted down with goodies, start slowly out the gate. There are two guys in it. As they approach the Dead Zone they drive, almost intentionally, right over our piano wire and beer bottles, knowing full well now that they're harmless. *Probably pissing them off!* They're certainly taking their time coming over, which gives me pause, but right now at this range if there's something else going on then these two geniuses are dead. The real reason is probably that their hearts just aren't into it. *Poor babies!*

A couple of minutes later and they pull up exactly where we want them to, and they're making a point of putting the Jeep right on the spot where it looks like the road *exactly* meets the cornfield. Almost as if they're saying "*Here assholes. Right where you asked. Anything else you want us to do? Fuck you!*" I get it. They got beat. Pretty badly. We're taking a lot of stuff from them. At gunpoint. It's humiliating. It's violating. They want to rebel against it, but it won't work. Rolling over and giving it up is *a big cock to swallow*. Especially if you're a warrior. But the greater good, that of the colony, should trump all else and make these tough guys here accept it and move on. The great ones do. It's tough though, I know. Remember Chupacabra-

Sniper's on the driver and Tommy's on Shotgun. Any weird move and these guys die. They shut down the Jeep.

I'm looking at the driver now, and he says, in that fake, complimentary voice "You look pretty good for a dead guy." So, as I suspected, *actually hoped*, this is the Whack-a-Mole who shot me. *Geez he's got balls!* You gotta love it.

"Yeah, thanks. I actually look really good as an alive guy too!"

My guys start laughing, and my friend here just keeps smiling.

"Green Beret?"

"Yup."

"Knew it. You're pretty goddamned good." Had me worried-"

"Had you dead!"

This guy sure is a cocky son of a bitch, I'll give him that. *The hair on the back of my neck is moving a little . . .*

"Thought you had me, but obviously you didn't. You outfoxed me with that one little desperation move, but I'm always ready for them. That's the difference." Compliment time is over. I can see it's bugging the crap out of him that he's on the shit end of this stick.

"You tired of living in that cage over there? Why don't you come ride with us? Get out and about the countryside, have some fun like we just had here, get to really do your thing, instead of playing nursemaid and security guard to a bunch of pilgrims."

"My wife's in there."

"Well hell, bring her along too! And any other young women who are looking for some real life adventure!"

So now Shotgun chimes in with "Hey man hold on! You're not taking any women!"

"He speaks," I say. "Listen boy, I didn't say we were taking anybody. I asked your friend here to see if anybody wanted to come along, so calm down." My voice has gotten really, *really* quiet again, and as I've mentioned before, this usually makes my crew nervous. *They've seen this movie before.*

"But listen up and remember, 'cause you won't ever hear it again—If I *wanted* to take anybody, *including* any of your women, there wouldn't be a goddamned fucking thing you could about it except shit on yourself, or die."

The words just hung there in the air, now in the midst of dead silence. My eyeballs have just about drilled a hole in this boy's skull, and I can tell he's feeling the heat, his Adam's apple's taking just the slightest bob.

"Now both you guys get out and unload all of the supplies. Open all the ammo canisters, the water container, all of it, keep it out for inspection."

They get to work. Mr. Green Beret is sneering at me, but they remove every packet, every package, wrap and unwrap, pour out all of the ammo cans, fill them back up again. I make them dump the wine barrel, which surprised them. *I guess we look thirsty.* The stuff is spread out all over the edge of the logging road. Then I make them remove the seats, dash and console from the jeep, while Mike inspects it from underneath. No hacksaw marks, no cut brakes, etc. etc. No signs of any explosives. For good measure I make Mr. Green Beret take the Jeep for a really hard spin up the road and around the Dead Zone, as torturous as he can make it on the Jeep. It doesn't blow apart, or up. We check it out under the hood, under the engine, make them overflow the fuel tank, looking for a charge when the key turns. It all looks pretty good. Now we make them put the Jeep back together and then pack up all the supplies and load them back into the Jeep again. Everything is good. I had already wrapped up the dogs, and had them load them carefully in the Jeep as well. This whole process took just about three hours, with only some minor grumbling from the Green Beret and Mr. Shotgun.

"Well ok guys, thanks very much for all the help. How many other jeeps you have anyway?" I asked, amusingly.

"Three," the Green Beret says.

"How many dogs left?"

"Three."

"I figured as much, on both counts. We're almost done. Where's the Dobie?"

"That's the one thing you can't have."

Silence, again—Hmmm. Now why of all things, including ammo, would this be the one thing that sticks like sand in their craw-

"And why would that be?"

"'Cause he's mine."

Well, that figures! A perfect, highly-trained dog raised by a Green Beret! More respect for that dog now.

"So you expect, I guess, some kind of professional courtesy from me, one warrior to another, to let you keep your dog?"

"Yeah, I was hoping you might see it that way-"

Well, there it is again, folks. *Hope*. The crack in the armor.

"Well, son, and I never got your name, by the way-"

"Trey"

"Well Trey, I agree with you. I have a lot of respect for Warriors of all types, for those who take on what others faint over."

"That's great, thanks."

"But I'm taking the dog anyway."

"Wait! What the fuck!'

"Sorry. Call for the dog now or Shotgun here takes the bullet. Then you. Your call."

"You fucking cocksucker!"

"Asshole, maybe. Murderer, possibly. Cocksucker, no, never. I'll leave that to your wife-" My voice goes quiet again. "Call the dog, Trey."

"CALL HIM TREY!" Shotgun is officially shitting his pants.

FWEEEEEHHHH. FWEEEEEHHHHHHH. This whistle is shrill, but loud and long-ranging. That dumb-ass gate lumbers open again and the Dobie comes hauling-ass out at about 25mph, sprinting right at us-

"Get him under control, Trey."

"BAYLOR! BAYLOR!" Trey's calling him now.

The dog closes the last hundred yards in about 6 seconds, comes sliding screeching stopping up to Trey, licking his face, jumping, spinning, happy to see his Master. A beautiful, *perfect* Doberman!

"You go to Baylor?" I ask.

"Fuck you. Take the dog. Get out. Don't come back."

Man! I keep trying to be friendly, but apparently my charm has left me.

"OK Trey. We're done. Gone. We're leaving, for now. If we feel like it, we'll be back in a year."

"C'mon boys, let's go. Baylor, C'mon boy!" The dog hesitates, but I'm cajoling him now with beef jerky. He jumps up in the shotgun seat of the Jeep.

"Good boy!" I'm feeding him Jerky. Mike starts driving the Jeep slowly away, the rest of us walking slowly behind, eyes like lasers on Trey and Shotgun.

I turn and start following the Jeep. *Geez, I'm glad this one's over. Toughest one so far, but I knew we'd win. I'm starting to feel that little high from the victory now!* We're gonna put on the dog tonight, pull out the Jack Daniels and . . .

"You realize this ain't over."

Whoa, wait now-

It's Trey, of course. He's got balls, but small brains. I turn in a split second and as I do the CZ-75 COMES UP I SNAP THE TRIGGER *BOOOM!!* THE BACK OF TREY's HEAD EXPLODES SHITTING BRAINS AND BLOOD ALL OVER SHOTGUN who recoils in horror, screaming, now on his knees, *wailing*. I sprint over in a heartbeat pull Shotgun up and *bitch-slap* him across the face "THE ONLY FUCKING REASON YOU ARE ALIVE IS TO DELIVER THIS MESSAGE: IT'S OVER! TREY WOULDN'T LET IT GO HE's FUCKING DEAD ANYONE ELSE COMES LOOKING WE BURN THIS FUCKING PLACE TO THE GROUND CAPECE?!!!

Shotgun's nodding, wailing, *oh shit* now vomiting as well.

It didn't have to end this way. Really. It was over. Trey, though, being the true warrior he was, couldn't live with it. He just couldn't keep his mouth shut. Sooner or later he might have convinced them all that he should come hunting us. *Can't have that!* Sometimes, as I've said before, it takes *more* balls to realize you've been beat, walk away, and take something from it. I guess Trey's balls weren't that big.

A man's got to know his limitations.

Whew! That was a long one! I guess it had to be because it was such a much bigger operation.

Hope you enjoyed reading that story as much as I enjoyed writing it. If you take a good hard look, from beginning to end it has all the elements of the other takedown scenarios, and follows much of the same logic as in my true personal stories. It's played out on a much bigger scale, of course, and in a much shorter timeframe.

Breaking down what you just read would take a whole 'nother 40 pages, so let's just skip to the high points. You should have been able to see all of my aforementioned 10-steps and other elements to a successful takedown unfold as you were reading it. Feel free to go back and see if you missed anything.

- First and foremost, *Recon*. This time it really counted, as we uncovered deadly tripwires, elevated shooting positions, etc. This helped us come to the conclusion that there was at least one Green Beret onsite, which forced us to change our plans. And he still almost got me!

- Gallons and gallons of blue paint. How many times have I brought this up throughout the book! It really mattered here as we were up against some deadly guys and the situation became tentative and fluid on multiple occasions.

- Weapons, weapons, weapons. We were as well-armed as they were, probably better-armed. We also had a few non-conventional weapons, like the Molotovs, which set the cornfield on fire, the tear gas, of course, and let's not forget our "IED string." Fooled them with that one.

- Staging. *It was perfect.* From our shooting positions, to our internal communications, to layer upon layer of tactics, through the implementation of our attack plans, we had it worked out perfectly. Pay attention to these details.

- Knowing your limitations. We were tested almost to the limit of ours. Trey certainly didn't know his.

- *Shit Happens!* All the time, everywhere. I got shot after misjudging the situation.

- Balls. Big ones. We have them, *do you?*

So Where Do We Go From Here?

We've obviously covered a lot of ground and lots of different types of material along the way, so maybe this is the right place to kick back and review what's gone on in the last 180 pages or so-

SUMMARY

In case you forgot, I kicked off this thing by getting passionate about the fact that being a "Doomsday Prepper" will most certainly bring about Doomsday for you. They are sheep on the way to slaughter, and I *damn* the industry that supports and feeds off their feeble minds!

I highlight in vivid detail what will happen right after a fall of civilized society, the horror, death, disease, rape, murder, psychosis.

Then I address the unlucky crowd that makes it past the first few days. How do you find water? How do you find food? How will you treat illness, injury, etc.?

And then the unspoken truth—if you manage to successfully address those issues, somebody or *bodies* will come and take it from you. Probably killing you in the process.

I *implore* you to become a Marauder. Learn to identify what you need or want, locate it, then go take it. I show you how to get your mind right, how to psychologically and physically prepare. How to get your gameface on, stockpile necessary items to get going, up your education and knowledge level appropriate to what you'll need when the time comes.

I then take you on a little detour through one of the defining moments in my past, to give you a framework as to how you might approach, think, and attempt to control a situation that looks virtually hopeless. *There is always a way!*

We then take a good long run through the Marauder Toolkit, everything you need to make it after the Fall. Important stuff, like guns, armor, chemicals, ammo, etc.

Then we kick the whole approach off in Marauding 101, with an initial set-up by the musings of some famous and notorious people. From there I walk you through the technical approach to marauding, the 10 Steps, psychological warfare, etc.

Around and through another detour into my personal life from the past, 'The Road To Leon,' detailing an operation which clearly outlines my 10 step process. *A great read as well!*

Then we eased into the actual *marauding* part of this book, by taking out a lightly defended farm, then moving onto a more heavily defended ranch.

I take you back into my past again, and tell a *little* story, "The Belly of the Sexy Beast," that has a *big* moral to it. One I come back to time and time again.

You all then pester the shit out of me until I go after some really big fish, a well-planned survivor colony that has some military attached to it. We battle that one out over almost 40 pages, but all along the way you can see my thought process, preparation, planning, tactics, *changes,* attitudes, moods, mood swings, injuries, loss—everything you will face when you get out there in that new world and start doing this kind of crap.

And here we are. So before I tack THE END onto this lumpy piece of firewood, let me outline for you what I think the most important Lessons Learned are that I hope you've taken from this book. There are many many things you can take away, of course, but without getting too technical I suggest the following:

RANDOM THOUGHTS ABOUT LESSONS LEARNED

1. Grow some balls.
2. Feel some fear. Deal with it.
3. Get in shape, physically and mentally.
4. Get some equipment, learn how to use it.
5. Learn about handguns and rifles. Take them apart and put them back together. *In your sleep.*
6. Learn how to shoot. Practice. Go hunting, kill something and eat it. It's not that bad.
7. Learn to ride a horse.
8. Read "The Anarchist's Cookbook."
9. In the next life, shoot first. *Then leave.*
10. Anything that can go wrong will go wrong.
11. Kill anyone you don't trust. *Immediately.*
12. Never take on SEALs or Marines straight-up
13. You can't run in the middle of a firefight. Avoid them.

14. RECONRECONRECONRECONRECON RECONRECON RECONRECONRECONRECONRECON RECON 'til you vomit.
15. *Pull the fucking trigger already!*
16. Feel free to use this book for ideas
17. Adapt or die.
18. *USE BLUE*
19. Kick back and enjoy the victories. I suggest Jack Daniels.
20. *Know your limitations!*

There you go. Happy Hunting!
Kilkenny-

HOW TO SURVIVE THE INITIAL POST-FALL CHAOS

The bulk of this book is dedicated to building a life in the afterlife that is primarily based out in the wide-open countryside, at best, or somewhere in the suburbs of a big city at worst. But what if you're an urban dweller, or you're stuck in a big city when everything goes to Hell, without warning? If you are in the general location of your home base (the same state), well, then the logical thing to do is to get back to it. If you're pretty far away and really have no hope of getting back to it, well then you're going to have to start from scratch. The worst place to be, of course, is stuck in a high-rise hotel in a big city.

Imagine something like the opening of world War Z, for example, or what went on in New Orleans during Hurricane Katrina. There is flat-out panic in the streets, complete breakdown of society, no help, no law, the only rule is Look Out For Yourself—*How the Hell do you do that?*

I'll show you how-

Remember, the objective is to get out of the city and on the way back to your home. If you are too far away from home, then the objective is still to get out of the city, but to make your way into the country, and start taking stuff early on while the things you need might still be available in order to get you started in the new world as a marauder. Listen up, it ain't gonna be easy—surviving this initial descent into anarchy will probably be the biggest fight you'll *ever* get into, in that next life or any other. If it happens to you, well, *good luck!*

HELL ON EARTH

Ok, so you have a little bit of a hangover from those shots with your buddies last night. You wake up about noon, on Saturday, turn on the TV, and nothing. Your cell phone has no service. Then you realize that your apartment has no power. You hear yelling coming from the 4th floor hallway outside the door in your apartment building, so you peek out and see your elderly neighbor yelling at her husband not to forget cat food. It seems the entire population of the 6 floors above you is pouring down the staircase into the street. *What's Happening*! You ask the old lady and she says that Washington DC has been destroyed in a nuclear attack. *What the fuck, am I still drunk?* The electric grid has failed. Nobody knows why. "People are going crazy," she says.

You run back inside and over to the bedroom window on the back side, take a look down below and there it is:

The initial onset of panic hits after the realization that this place is *fucked!* and no help is coming. Looting is rampant, cars are jamming the streets, masses of people are running everywhere, hysterical—*My head is killing me!* Hopefully you have a case or two of water, soda or beer back up here in your apartment, maybe some bags of chips, cookies, chocolates or other munchies and carbs too.

So now what?

Like everyone else, grab a pillow case, plastic garbage bag, jacket, hoodie whatever and head to the nearest supermarket, *fast!* then stuff it full of junk food carbohydrates, power bars and Beef Jerky. As much as you can. Let everyone else go for the other stuff. Eventually you're going to be on the move with this stuff in a backpack, and that packaged carbo stuff and beef jerky weigh almost nothing. Next, the tougher stuff—get some individual water bottles, coke cans, whatever, anything you can drink and as much as you can carry. Then take lots of Purell. Head over to the pharmacy and start ripping out Zithromax, Cipro, Penicillin, Amoxicillin, any antibiotic you can think of, although they might be gone by the time you get there. Anywhere you can find Ibuprofen, advil, motrin, etc., take it. All of this will keep you going a few weeks. Get back to your apartment.

The temptation at this point may be to unload, get back down to the street and start re-loading food and water supplies again. *Forget that!* You have enough supplies for a couple of weeks now, if you're smart. This post-fall panic will subside, the shelves will empty, then people will scatter into hiding, and everything will turn to fear. Before that happens, you need to think about *defending yourself.* If you have a gun, great. Go get more ammo. If you don't have a gun, well, now's the time to go get one, before the opportunity slips away . . .

Okay, put on some ragged clothes, or tear up and dirty up something you're already wearing. Make yourself look like some kind of victim. Grab a couple of serrated-edge steak knives and grip one closely in each hand. One blade-up, the other blade-down. Head out, *fast!*

Talk to no one, *run*. Slice anybody who slows you. *You must be single-minded and unstoppable in this task.* The most likely place to get a gun is not at a gun shop, even if you know where one is and there's one nearby, as they will all be gone by the time you get there. **The most likely place to get a gun is from a cop.** If there is total panic in the city, at some point the individual cops will give it up and start taking care of themselves as well. *You must find a cop.* This will be your hardest task, trust me. When you do, *Surprise and Deception will be your best tools*—You already look like a victim, so plead to him for help. The cop will refuse to do anything, as his world, too, has gone to shit, and he's thinking about his wife, kids, girlfriend whatever so when he turns to go you immediately choke-hold and take him to the ground, if you don't want to kill him. In 6-9 seconds he will be unconscious. If you don't think you are physically or mentally capable of this, then you'll just have to slit his throat.

Too brutal for you? Then run home, take a crap and await Death!

Remember now, this is in a scenario where there is no law. People will be coming for you. Coming for your stuff, food, water. They will take your wife, girlfriend, whatever, if you

DOOMSDAY MARAUDERS

have any. You want this? *Then go home and wait for it, as you will surely get it.*

Immediately grab his gun before others come for it. Once secured, grab the extra magazines and ammunition. Then, and only then, grab his taser as well, and if he's wearing armor, strip it and go. If others come swarming, just leave with the gun. Now you can roam about and see what's left on the shelves, in a little bit less of a panic, as you're probably holding a Glock 17 or something similar, and even if you can't shoot it, you'll hold the bad guys off. Congratulations. *Now you're a Marauder-*

Ok, well, you've been hiding out at home for a couple of days, waiting around, hoping that something will magically change out there on the streets. *You should have been gone already, now it's only going to get tougher* — Many of the tenants have left already, but the building is still about half-full. Your elderly neighbors are in bad shape, as the old man wasn't able to bring anything home. He was beaten badly by a bunch of kids just outside the food store. The kids took the cat food as well. They're just about out of water too.

You've officially arrived at a *chokepoint*. This is the time and place where you make the move, *or not*. You have enough food to last a few weeks, holed-up in your apartment. Maybe enough water (coke, beer, etc.), if you ration it properly, for 10 days or so. You can shit in a plastic bag and toss it out the window, as the plumbing is out, then use lots of Purell. Okay, cool. So what happens in 10 days? You go out looking for water then? What about the old folks across the hall? Do you share with them and knock it down to four days? Then what? Really, you have to make a decision!

Ok, I'll make it for you—*Get the fuck out! Now! You've wasted too much time already! The safest time to leave was right during the initial panic! Now there's gangs roaming the streets, some with guns, some without, all with trouble written on their foreheads. They're burning everything in sight and raiding apartment buildings just like yours. It probably won't be more than a few more days before they get around to your neighborhood!*

Ok, Ok, I've convinced you. You've finally decided to leave . . . Now you need to get organized for the *start* of the rest of your new life-

Hopefully by now you've taken a complete inventory of all of the materials in your apartment, especially in the kitchen. Lucky you, there's Drano, Liquid Plumr, Oven Cleaner, Bleach, plastic bottles, aluminum cans and glass bottles as well. A whole box of Aluminum foil. *Nice.* The problem you have now is how much of all this can you physically carry. I suggest Coke cans first (you may need that sugar and caffeine), packages of beef jerky next (protein acts as a dirty carbohydrate when necessary) then the high-carb foods last. Painkillers and antibiotics right behind. A couple of pairs of socks, a couple of extra underwear. Pack a pair of light sneakers, wear a solid pair of hiking shoes or running shoes. Then pack your household chemicals, if you can carry them. At least a little bit of each.

DOOMSDAY MARAUDERS

Dangerous gangs of looters and raiders are still roaming about the streets, so it's probably safer to hole up in your apartment until dark, tonight, then make your way out. *Keep that Glock cocked and locked!*

The elderly neighbors are really suffering now. The old man has been lapsing into unconsciousness frequently since the beating, and he's not eating much at all. His wife is not much better; she's very weak from the water rationing, worry over her husband, and the realization that this will be a *slow torturous end to their once-happy lives. The cats are licking their chops in anticipation.* Fortunately, the old lady has been giving her husband a little bit of Dilaudid, a prescription synthetic morphine painkiller, from a prescription she had after hip surgery a year earlier . . .

So you're packed and ready to go now, one backpack, 35 pounds worth of Coke, water, beef jerky, peanut butter, crackers, bleach, Drano, oven cleaner, foil etc. etc. A flashlight for good measure, but you're not going to use it tonight and light yourself up as a target! Just about dark, getting anxious, it's almost time to go. You head back over to the old folks across the hall, and the old man is sitting up in bed, awake, but barely. His wife sits next to him on the bed as well. You tell them that you heard in the street that the Army has come and is attempting to restore order again! It should only be a matter of a few days before emergency services start flowing again! This calls for a celebration! Let's use up some of our supplies! Smiles, some mild laughing, and obvious relief on the old folks' worn faces; A cup of tea would have been perfect for these two but as there's no working stove, a good old-fashioned alcoholic beverage will have to do. You brought a bottle of Cabernet with you, and as you go rummaging around their kitchen looking for a corkscrew, you locate the dilaudid and crush the remaining pills into powder. These pills are very, very tiny, as they are very, very powerful. "Found the corkscrew!" You pour a small amount of Cab into their glasses, adding the Dilaudid powder. You have Coke in your glass. Back to their bedroom. "A toast," you say, "to making it all the way through." Smiles from both, weak, but real. Also a sense of relief as well. They'll both be fine now. You start talking about what you all are going to do when the world rights itself again, take a cruise, go to Italy. You say that all you want is a good hot bath! Slow laughing, then yawns. The old man is falling asleep. His wife says she's tired as well. You tuck them both in bed together, tell them you'll be back to check on them in a few hours, and say goodbye. They've now stopped breathing-

Ok heading out into the dark hallway down the stairs and OH SHIT THERE'S LOOTERS IN THE STAIRWELL ON THE LOWER FLOORS SMASHING IN DOORS SCREAMING SOME GUNSHOTS THEY'RE MOVING UP!!!

OK back into the apartment. You're going to have to go out the window to get down four storeys to the street. *Jesus fucking Christ!* But that's not the problem. The problem is *can you do it before the gangs get there?*

You go find a vacuum cleaner cord, an extension cord, any long length of power cord. Don't cut off the plugs or receptacle ends. Tie it together for as long as you need to reach the street. When tying them together, make sure you tie a "square knot" each time, as power cords can be slippery. The intact plug ends protect against this, however. Tie a knot in the cords every 10 feet. Secure one end around a strong part of the infrastructure, like the radiators, plumbing, etc., by tying one end around a metal cylindrical item (bat, pipe, etc.), then square knotting the cylindrical end around the secure fixture. The cylinder is added protection against slippage.

*You can hear smashing and screaming on the floor below you. They're coming. You're almost done tying the length of the vacuum cleaner and extension cords together. Screaming, another gunshot below. Hurry Goddamit! More smashing of doors, painful screaming. What are they doing? You run over and peek out your door, the raiders are literally a flight of stairs below you, getting ready to move on up. This is another **chokepoint**; act now or die.*

Ok into the backpack, pull out the drano. Half a bottle into an empty plastic container you put in the trash. Rip up a bunch of aluminum foil . . . open your apartment door . . . rush over to the top of the staircase, you can see them on the floor below . . . stuff the foil into the plastic bottle half-filled with Drano . . . screw the cap on tight . . . shake it up a little . . . toss it down the stairs . . .

The raiders see you and start up after you then BBOOOOOMM! The Drano bomb explodes, showering them with boiling lye and poisonous fumes! Now they're screaming in horror and pain, and are running back downstairs. Perfect! You've bought some time!

You go find some kitchen gloves, work gloves or winter gloves, don the backpack and toss the cord out the back window opposite the side of the building that the raiders occupy. Slide feet out first, facing the building. Don't worry, it's pitch black outside, nobody sees you. Get your feet flat on the wall, push back and out, in a squat, and walk backwards down the wall. The knots every ten feet or so will help stop any potential slippage. At a leisurely pace you can cover 100 feet in 60 seconds.

A minute and a half later you're on the ground. Glock in hand. Don't waste ammo, but if you come across anyone who tries to approach you, they're not looking for friends. *Shoot them and keep going.* Hopefully you have an idea where you're heading, I can't help you with that. Just do what you can to get there. The rest will take care of itself. *Welcome to my world! You're now well on your way toward an exciting new career!*

Okay, Okay, one more for the road . . .

THAT GIRL IN THE BAR IN BOGOTA'

In our relentless pursuit of the Cartel we employed many tactics, of course, and an important one was "follow the money trail." Easy to do once you're on it, but not so easy to find it and even harder to get on it once you do locate it. That involves guys with huge balls (DEA) and putting certain individuals with small brains (me) at great risk.

Always a smiling optimist, I am up to the task (or it just doesn't register as to how ridiculously stupid I am). My international banking activity in Colombia, Mexico and Argentina has given me a certain visibility, which is always good-news bad-news. Good news—*Wealth! Hot Babes!* Bad news—*Two snatch attempts*! Snatch attempts give you great street cred, though, as they certainly weren't staged, no, uh-uh for real these guys wanted to ransom me. The Cartel knows the guys trying to pull this off and that it's not bullshit, so they know I'm for real, and as I had survived both attempts, probably tougher than most, and a little more savvy than most of the other pussy bankers hanging out down there. They see the money I throw around down there and think *maybe I'm a little* dirty and somebody they can do business with. They need someone like me, *a money launderer.* They have too much physical cash, hundreds of millions of actual individual dollar bills that they can't spend, and it's getting hard to protect. That is a shitload of paper! *That's my route to the trail.*

So of course Uncle Sam couldn't be happier when I got hit on *again* by one of those unbelievably smoking hot Colombian "prostitutes" in the bar at my hotel, the Tequendama, in Bogota.' *Even today Obama's own Secret Service can't resist them!* Think on a scale of 1-10 that Sofia Vergara is a 5 and this chick is a *9! Unfortunately,* this story is not about her—*encourage me* and I might write that one another time! I did take the bait though, and set up my first real contact with the Cartel-

Sorry, just kidding! You'll have to wait for the next book!
K

ABOUT THE AUTHOR

Kilkenny is a former U.S. Intelligence operative and successful International Banker. Born and raised in the Bronx, Kilkenny played football for Boston College and graduated with a degree in International Economics. A very involved father of three, he currently splits his time between a suburban Los Angeles home and his sprawling Colorado ranch, with his beautiful wife Sarah and a bunch of skeletons in the closet.

CPSIA information can be obtained
at www.ICGtesting.com
Printed in the USA
LVOW08s0531200717
541958LV00001B/122/P